*E*mily scanned the paddock, looking to the left in time to see a little shadow dart around the corner and out of sight.

She started after him. "You do realize that I'm here to give you treats, don't you?" she called out. "And I'm going to brush you and get all the snarls and mud out of your coat, and you'll feel wonderful." She rounded the corner and stopped abruptly at the sight of him.

The little pony was backed into a corner, his head up, his eyes wide, his nostrils flaring, as if she were some great enemy come to do him harm. His front feet were splayed, and his thick white mane almost completely covered his face. His mane spilled over all sides of his neck, nearly down to his chest. His coat, from what she could see beneath the mud, was a rich gold. A classic palomino and completely cute.

And apparently terrified of her.

Her heart tightened and she held out a carrot, crooning softly. "Hey, little man, you're not at that awful place anymore. You're safe now. It's okay."

Read all the books in the
RUNNING HORSE RIDGE series

HEATHER BROOKS

Running Horse Ridge

Hercules: A Matter of Trust

HarperTrophy®
An Imprint of HarperCollins*Publishers*

Running Horse Ridge #2: Hercules: A Matter of Trust
Copyright © 2009 by HarperCollins Publishers
All rights reserved. Printed in the United States of America.
No part of this book may be used or reproduced in any manner whatsoever
without written permission except in the case of brief quotations embodied
in critical articles and reviews. For information address HarperCollins
Children's Books, a division of HarperCollins Publishers, 1350 Avenue of
the Americas, New York, NY 10019.
www.harpercollinschildrens.com

Library of Congress Cataloging-in-Publication Data
Brooks, Heather.
      Hercules: A matter of trust / Heather Brooks. — 1st ed.
          p.   cm. — (Running Horse Ridge ; #2)
      Summary: Emily must learn to trust her Aunt Debby in order to
feel comfortable at the family's horse ranch and rescue center, just as a
terrified pony must learn to trust people in order to be rehabilitated.
      ISBN 978-0-06-142981-1 (pbk. bdg.)
      [1. Horses—Fiction.   2. Trust—Fiction.   3. Aunts—Fiction.
4. Ponies—Fiction.   5. Animal sanctuaries—Fiction.]   I. Title.
PZ7.B7943Mat   2009   2008036463
[Fic]—dc22   CIP
                                                              AC

Typography by Amy Ryan
❖
First Edition

Hercules: A Matter of Trust

1

*E*mily Summers was on her knees in the main aisle of the Running Horse Ridge barn trimming Sapphire's ankles, and she couldn't stop giggling.

She was peering intently at Sapphire's left front hoof as she carefully glided the electric clippers over the glossy black hair, when she felt something nuzzling her back pocket for the fifth time.

She peeked over her left shoulder at Sapphire's dark brown eyes blinking innocently at her, even as his upper lip was trying to worm the piece of carrot out of her jeans. "I already told you, that's not yours. The fifteen I already gave you are all you're getting!"

He stopped nibbling on her jeans, his dark face

with the white blaze so close that she couldn't resist the urge to give him a little kiss right on the splash of white between his eyes. He immediately lifted his upper lip and grinned at her, then gave her a firm nudge with his nose that knocked her right over onto the rubber mat they were standing on.

Emily laughed as Sapphire pressed his face to her chest, wiggling his black ears as if to point out no one was scratching them. She smiled and scratched behind his ears, and he let out a loud sigh of satisfaction, blowing hay dust across the floor. "You do realize you are so making it hard to get anything accomplished, don't you?"

He snuffled against her, and she realized he was trying to lick her jeans, searching for any remnants of anything tasty, as he'd done ever since he'd found chocolate ice cream on her pants the first time they'd met.

And yes, okay, so maybe she'd intentionally spilled ice cream on her jeans a couple times since then just because she thought it was so cute the way he licked it off. . . .

"Emily!"

Emily scrambled to her feet at the sound of her aunt's voice, brushing the hay off her pants. Had her aunt caught her allowing Sapphire to knock her down?

She hoped not. She and her aunt had very different ideas about what Sapphire should be allowed to do, and since Aunt Debby owned him, she got to make the rules.

And her aunt didn't appreciate it when Emily broke them, as Emily knew all too well. She didn't *try* to break the rules, really; she didn't. It just . . . well, sometimes it just happened.

Wiping her hands on her jeans, she turned to face her aunt. "Hi, Aunt Debby."

Aunt Debby was wearing jeans and worn paddock boots as she always did. Her gray T-shirt had the family farm's name across the front in letters that were so faded Emily could barely read them. Aunt Debby's light brown hair was pulled up in a ponytail that showed her silver hoop earrings. She set her hands on her hips and raised her brows.

Emily winced. Oh, Aunt Debby had so seen Emily allow Sapphire to goof around.

"Where are the cross ties?" Aunt Debby asked.

Emily quickly grabbed a cross tie and hooked it to Sapphire's halter. "If I cross-tie him, then he can't reach my jeans to lick them—"

"Of course he can't. That's the point. We're trying to train him so he can be sold." Aunt Debby hooked up the other cross tie and gave Sapphire a pat.

"But he gets so bored—" Emily swallowed her protest at Aunt Debby's look. "Yeah, okay," she mumbled, hating the mention of Sapphire being sold.

Yes, she'd known Sapphire only for a few weeks, but the thought of being at Running Horse Ridge without him . . . Somehow in the short time she'd been at the farm, he'd become more important to her even than Rhapsody, the horse she was leasing back home in New Jersey.

Emily instantly felt guilty about Rhapsody. She loved him, too. She did. But he wasn't there and Sapphire was and Sapphire needed her and—

There was a soft snort behind her, and she turned her head to see Max, the old gray horse who got the run of the farm, standing in the aisle behind her. "Max!" He'd been following her around lately, and she suspected it was because he missed Grandpa. From what her family had told her, Max and Grandpa had been best friends until Grandpa had died, and Max hadn't been quite himself ever since. She handed Max the one piece of carrot she'd held back from Sapphire. "Here you go, sweetie. I had to fight Sapphire off for it, so appreciate it."

Max gently took the hunk of carrot between his lips while Sapphire perked his ears and watched the old horse as if he was hoping for a stray piece to drop to the floor. When nothing seemed forthcoming, Sapphire set his chin on Emily's shoulder with a resigned grunt. Max's eyes studied Emily and Sapphire, his jaw moving slowly as he worked his way through the carrot.

Aunt Debby patted Max's neck. "That's nice you're befriending Max. I think he's lonely." There was a softness in her voice that made Emily glance at her aunt. She'd only seen her aunt be that gentle once, when a horse they'd both loved had died.

Aunt Debby was smiling at the old guy, her gaze warm with concern. Emily knew from the look on Aunt Debby's face that Max would never have to worry about being sold. Aunt Debby might be all business when it came to training Sapphire, but there was only love when she looked at Max. Emily felt a tinge of jealousy. Aunt Debby had never looked at Emily like that, even though they were family. . . . Whoa. Since when was she jealous of a horse? That was *ridiculous.*

Emily gave Max's withers a brisk scratch. "Yeah, I think he's lonely, too." Emily wrinkled her nose at the dirt under her fingernails when she lifted her hand from Max's coat. "I'll give him a bath today, and then a good brushing." She cooed at him, "You'd like that, wouldn't you, old guy? Maybe we could get Caitlyn to help."

Caitlyn was Emily's seven-year-old cousin. Totally sweet and nice, Caitlyn was the only one at Running Horse Ridge who had made Emily feel welcome from the first moment she'd arrived.

Well, Caitlyn and Sapphire.

Aunt Debby's soft look faded from her face. Her eyes became serious, suddenly all business again. "Later you may be too busy to pamper Max."

Emily cocked her head, not certain how to interpret her aunt's statement. Was she in trouble for something? She'd been working so hard to prove herself to her aunt, to show she was worthy of being trusted with the animals even though she came from a dressage barn and . . . um . . . yeah, okay, even though she'd stolen Sapphire and nearly lost him and had almost broken her own ankle. . . .

She wrapped her arm around Sapphire's head, pleased that he still hadn't lifted his chin from her shoulder. She rested her cheek against his, the fine black hairs so soft against her skin. He snuffled softly, and some of her tension eased as she looked at her aunt. "What's up?"

"How's your ankle?"

Emily flexed the ankle, testing it. There was a slight twinge, but her tightly laced paddock boots immobilized the ankle well, as did the lace-up booty thing that the doctor had given her after he'd taken the cast off a couple days ago. "Feels fine."

"No problems after the lesson yesterday?"

"Nope." Emily had had another jumping lesson on Moondance yesterday, her second one. It had been as fun as the first lesson, and she'd even managed not to fall off, which was a definite step up after her first jumping lesson. It was a little daunting because she wasn't nearly as good at jumping as she was at dressage, and Emily knew that Aunt Debby and everyone else at Running Horse Ridge respected only hunter/jumper riders, not dressage.

Which was why she had to learn how to jump: so that Aunt Debby would trust her and let her ride Sapphire. Emily wasn't worried about her skills, though. She was a good enough dressage rider that mastering jumping would come without too much trouble, as long as she kept doing it. And if she fell off a few more times in the process? Totally worth it.

Emily noticed that her aunt's eyes were twinkling, almost as if she were hiding some big secret.

"I have a proposal for you," Aunt Debby said. "And Sapphire."

"For Sapphire?" Emily frowned, realizing that it

hadn't been a casual visit to Sapphire's stall at all. Her aunt had an agenda involving Sapphire.

And with him for sale, that was always a scary thing.

$\mathcal{E}$mily slid her hand around the slick leather of Sapphire's halter. "What kind of proposal?" she asked cautiously.

Aunt Debby grinned suddenly, as if she'd been trying to fake Emily out with her serious expression. "You interested in going to a horse show tomorrow?"

"What?" Emily blinked in surprise. "A *what*?"

"A horse show, silly. You know, where you ride horses and compete?" Aunt Debby was laughing now, clearly enjoying the fact she'd made Emily nervous.

"Oh my gosh! Really?" Emily did a little hop of excitement, making both horses jerk their heads back in surprise. "A dressage show is in town?"

"Dressage?" Aunt Debby looked confused for a second. "No, it's a hunter/jumper show. I was going to have you jump."

"No dressage?" The excitement whooshed right out of Emily. She'd been a dressage rider for years. No jumps, just very detailed and precise work on the flat. It was what she excelled at.

But her aunt's farm was a hunter/jumper barn that not only didn't do dressage, but they didn't even *respect* it. Not that Emily was against jumping. Her two jumping lessons had been a total blast, but well, she was sort of *bad* at jumping.

Well, not *bad* bad, but in comparison to her dressage skills, she was awful at jumping. But she *was* getting better, and it was so much fun. . . .

"Emily? Are you interested? The show's a couple hours away, which means we'll have to be driving out of here at about four thirty tomorrow morning."

Emily had a sudden vision of her alarm going off in the middle of the night, of the eager anticipation of leaping out of bed and racing to the barn, of riding into the ring before a judge, of competing. . . . Her heart started to race and her stomach fluttered with sudden excitement.

A show was still a show, and she'd missed three big

dressage shows since she and her dad had come out to Oregon a few weeks ago. The thought of getting back in the ring—too awesome! She let out a whoop of glee at the sudden rush of anticipation. "Oh, *yes* I'm so in! Can I ride Sapphire in the show?" She knew what the answer would be, but she asked anyway. "*Please?* Competing in shows is my specialty, you know. I used to compete every weekend back home, and I'm really good under pressure. I'd be so good for him—"

Aunt Debby chuckled and gave Emily an affectionate brush on the shoulder. "You never give up, do you?"

Emily nearly leaped in excitement at her aunt's laughter. She hadn't flat-out denied Emily's request to ride him! Did that mean Emily was making progress? That Aunt Debby was actually considering allowing Emily to ride him? Oh, *wow.* "Of course I'm not giving up! I'm trying to wear you down with Sapphire until you finally let me ride him just to shut me up. Is it working? Can I ride him in the show? *Please?*"

"No, you still aren't ready to ride him, but I admire the effort." Her aunt scratched Sapphire on his forehead, and the beautiful black horse stretched his head toward her. "But you can show him in a model class."

"Really? Really? *Really?*" Emily squealed and threw

herself on her aunt, giving her a huge hug. "I can really show him?"

Aunt Debby gave a loud bark of laughter this time. "Yes, you can."

"Wow. Wow! That's so cool." Emily released her aunt and flung her arms around Sapphire's muscular neck, squeezing as hard as she could. "Did you hear that, Sapphire? We get to show together. In a model class!"

Sapphire swung his head around to look at her, as if wondering what in the world she was getting so fired up about, and Emily suddenly realized she had no idea! She whirled toward her aunt. "What's a model class? If I'm not riding him, then how can I be showing him?"

Her aunt patted Max, who had shoved his way past Sapphire and was standing in the aisle next to Aunt Debby, swishing his tail impatiently. "It's where you lead him in and stand him up properly to show off his conformation, then trot him a bit to show his movement. He'll wear a bridle, but no saddle."

"Seriously?" Emil frowned, trying to picture a class where people just walked around leading their horses. All she got was an image of the Westminster dog show and the little fluffy white dogs strutting around. Sapphire acting like a fluffy dog? That was completely ridiculous!

"There's no riding at all? Is that a real class?"

"Yes, it's a real class, and it's a very important one for a horse as beautiful as Sapphire. It'll showcase him." They both turned to inspect Sapphire, who pricked his ears and returned their gazes with a curious expression.

Aunt Debby held up her fingers and fluttered them, and Sapphire lifted his head to watch them. "See how he has his ears up and his eyes are bright and focused?"

Emily nodded. "He looks majestic. Like a king." So not a fluff ball!

"That's exactly the look we want." Aunt Debby dropped her hand, and Sapphire nudged it to see if she'd been hiding anything in it. "You'll need to stand him so his front feet are even and one hind foot is about ten inches in front of the other. You should practice a bit."

Emily pursed her lips and rubbed Sapphire's nose, her stomach a little achy at the thought of going to a show so potential buyers would notice how beautiful Sapphire was. But if she didn't do it, would someone else get to? "Okay. I'll do it."

Aunt Debby continued talking as if she hadn't even considered that Emily might have refused. "And you'll ride Moondance in a couple classes as well. It will be a good experience for you."

Emily stared at her. "*Jumping?*" Did her aunt really

believe in her enough to let her jump in a show? "Really?"

"Of course." Aunt Debby raised her brows. "Unless you're not interested?"

Tears pricked at the back of Emily's eyes for a split second at the realization that her aunt was going to let her jump. That her aunt had that kind of faith in Emily, faith that Emily had worked *so hard* for. "Oh, *no*. I am *so* interested."

Aunt Debby nodded. "I figured you would be. So I'll need you to get both horses ready for the show. Baths, then trim them and clean their tack. You know how to braid?"

"I'm a great braider." Emily's heart was racing at the thought of going to a show with Sapphire, at the thought of jumping at a show. Jumping! How cool was that? "The best in my old barn."

"Great. You can do Moondance and Sapphire." Aunt Debby glanced at her watch. "I have to run, but there's a pony in the back paddock that I want to bring in and start to work with. He's one of the horses we rescued from Trooper's barn, but I haven't had time to do anything with him yet. He's a palomino Shetland. Do you think you'll have time to go grab him this afternoon and clean him up? One of the gals told me he seems skittish, so I need an idea of what his issues are. Let me know how it goes?" Aunt Debby rubbed the back of her hand over her forehead, suddenly looking weary. "There's so much to do with all these horses we recently rescued, and we've got to start working our way through them."

Another chance to show her aunt that she was responsible? To force her aunt to see her as someone mature enough to be trusted riding Sapphire, even though he was so spirited and so valuable? "You bet. What's his name?"

Aunt Debby shrugged. "No idea. Why don't you come up with one for him?"

"Cool!" Emily whirled back to Sapphire as Aunt Debby walked off. "We are so going to dominate!" She threw her arms over her head and did a quick jig in place. "And I'm going to ride Moondance and do so awesome that Aunt Debby will let me ride you from now on. This is *it*! It's our chance to show her that we belong together! Is this the best or *what*?"

Sapphire snorted and stomped his foot.

"I know! What are we doing chatting? We have work to do!" She grabbed the clippers and flipped them on, the familiar buzz whirring through the air. "We have to make you look beautiful, don't we? A little whisker trim is definitely needed." Sapphire dropped his head obligingly as she began trimming his whiskers, humming happily. . . .

"She's going to make you ride in the Maiden class."

Emily looked up at her younger cousin Kyle, who was lurking at the end of the aisle. She winced, remembering how the first time they'd met, he'd drenched her with his turbo squirt gun. He wasn't a *bad* kid, but he liked to tease his sisters, and he'd been happy to include Emily in his stable of victims. As if she wasn't already feeling weird being dumped in the middle of a big family after a lifetime of being only with her dad, Kyle had quickly made her realize that life without a younger brother had been a very good thing.

Kyle's Game Boy was clutched in his left hand, and he was wearing shredded jeans and a black T-shirt, like the renegade cop in the movie the family had watched last night, on Family DVD Night. Even though the movie had been bad, Emily had to admit it had been kind of fun hanging out with everyone, eating popcorn with extra butter and drinking homemade lemonade. It had also been sort of weird because everyone had been quoting the movie, which they'd apparently watched before, and Emily and her dad had been the only ones who hadn't been part of the joke so she'd felt a little left out.

She realized suddenly that Kyle was sporting the same smug smirk the movie cop had had when he'd been about to expose the bad guy. He was looking decidedly pleased. Too pleased. Like he'd found another way to torture her. "Did you hear me?" he asked. "I said my mom's going to make you ride in the Maiden class."

Emily frowned, watching him carefully to make sure he didn't have a squirt gun hidden behind his leg. One hand was hidden behind his back. "What are you talking about?"

"Maiden. It's the class for beginners. Even Caitlyn can't ride in Maiden classes anymore because once you win one, you're disqualified. Caitlyn's seven, and she rides in a higher class than you're going to be doing. Alison rides in the Open division because she's won so many she has to be in the top level."

Emily frowned at the mention of her older cousin. Alison might have more experience over fences, sure, but Emily knew she was a better rider. Better form, better understanding of how to really *ride*, even if Alison got to jump higher than Emily did. "I'm not a beginner—"

"Doesn't matter. You know how my mom is. You're going to be in Maiden for sure. That'll be fun to watch you lined up with all these kids that can barely stay in the saddle." Kyle moved suddenly, and Emily lunged for him, ripping the squirt gun from his fingers before he could get it out.

"Hey!" He shouted his protest as she turned the florescent orange gun on him and pumped it.

It *splooshed* right in his face, and he howled with rage and grabbed it out of her hand. "I can't believe you did that!"

Emily laughed as he pumped the empty barrel at her, getting nothing but a few drips that landed on the toes of his dirty sneakers. "Don't underestimate East Coast girls, Kyle. We're dangerous."

He scowled at her. "This is war."

She smiled brightly, amused by the wariness on his face. He was so afraid of her! "Bring it on. I'm ready."

He wrinkled his nose at her then spun around and stalked down the aisle, his gun clutched in his fingers, his feet squishing as the water dripped down his front. Emily wiped her wet hands on her jeans, grinning at Sapphire. "Then again," she told Sapphire, "maybe there's a reason for little brothers. It's kind of fun to beat them at their own game."

Kyle turned at the end of the aisle. "Beginner!" he yelled.

"I'm not—"

But he was already gone, his cackle echoing down the aisle as his sneakers squeaked on the cement floor.

Emily's elation faded as she stared after him, thinking about the image he'd drawn of her in a class with a bunch of six-year-olds. Aunt Debby wouldn't really make her enter a class with little kids, would she? Then she thought about Aunt Debby, and realized, yes, she really might. The clippers fell limply to her side, her shoulders drooping.

Oh, boy. That would be majorly humiliating. . . .

What would her friends in New Jersey say? She could hear their laughter, hear the snarky comments of Jenny Smith, saying she always knew she was really better than Emily. . . .

"No." Emily pulled back her shoulders and lifted her chin. She'd won so many dressage classes that surely she wouldn't be eligible for a Maiden class. Yes, she wasn't a star jumper *yet*, but surely she deserved the chance to at least compete against kids her own age, didn't she? She'd find Aunt Debby and explain. She and Aunt Debby would strategize like Emily always used to do with Les, her coach in New Jersey, before a show. Aunt Debby would respect Emily even more for her insight, and everything would work out fine.

Emily pursed her lips and grabbed a currycomb,

rubbing circles on Sapphire's coat while she made her plan. In New Jersey she and her best friend, Giselle, would always team up when they disagreed with Les's coaching decisions, and they almost always got him to see their point. Who could she get to approach Aunt Debby with her?

Her cousin Alison would be good. Aunt Debby respected Alison's riding and might listen to her. No. Alison had no respect for dressage and would never stand up for her.

Kyle? Emily snorted and smacked the currycomb on her thigh to shake off some of the dirt and hair. As if.

What about Uncle Rick? No, he was too busy with his veterinarian practice, plus he seemed to leave all the barn stuff to Aunt Debby.

It would have to be her dad. He'd ditched the farm for the last decade, but he was already making himself at home here. Surely Aunt Debby would listen to her own brother?

Then Emily thought about her dad and how he'd changed since they'd been there. Before they'd arrived on the farm a few weeks ago, she would have asked him knowing he'd stand by her no matter what.

But since their arrival, he'd started to change, siding with her aunt instead of Emily. And she knew he'd do the same in this case, deferring to Aunt Debby as if she were the queen of the place. Emily didn't come first for him anymore.

She frowned, realizing she didn't come first for *anyone* right now. At least, not enough to corral anyone into her corner against her aunt. Not like she did at home. At home she had her dad and Giselle and Les and . . .

Emily bit her lower lip and her eyes began to sting. Here . . . she was alone. In this huge family she was alone.

Sapphire nickered softly and pressed his nose against her side. She bit her lip and hugged him, burying her face in his shiny coat. "It doesn't matter," she said fiercely, gripping his mane tightly. "Who needs them? We don't." She could do this. She didn't need help. "I can manage my aunt, no problem."

Something hit her in the back, and she lifted her head to see Max standing behind her. He stomped his foot impatiently, and she slung one arm around his neck, too. "Why do I need people? I have you two. I don't need them."

But when she heard Alison's laughter echo in the air, followed by Aunt Debby's booming laugh, she realized she was lying to herself just a little bit.

Several hours later Emily had put Sapphire back in his stall, his whiskers neatly trimmed, as well as his ears and his feet. He looked beautiful and sharp, and his coat was gleaming from her rubdown. She'd actually rubbed him so hard her arm was sore, but she was determined to prove that she shouldn't be discounted. That she could belong here.

She'd eventually decided to try to get her dad to help her with Aunt Debby, but he'd gone to town to pick up some meds for the rescue horses, so she'd headed out to the back paddock to find the pony her aunt wanted her to bathe. Working with the rescued horses always put her in a better mood, because they were all so desperate for a little love that it made her feel awesome to give it to them.

Emily trucked along the path toward the back paddock, a halter and a lead shank draped over her shoulder. The path was dirt, but not too rocky, and there were green grass and bushes surrounding her. Oregon was so green Emily felt like she was in the Amazon rain forest, immersed in a world of lush vegetation.

She inhaled deeply as she walked, breathing in the scent of cool dampness from the rain they'd had the night before. Her feet sank in the soft dirt. Her paddock boot left behind a perfect footprint—like the earth was molding to her feet and leaving a trail for the world to find.

She lifted her head and gazed ahead at the vast expanse of fields before her, at the split rail fences protecting the horses from getting loose. At home, the one turnout pasture was a ring of bark dust and dirt. This was . . . She took a deep breath and smiled.

This turnout area was vast space where she could have the alone time she was used to, privacy that felt nonexistent with her family all around her. Not that she totally minded family, but when she was upset, she was used to being able to go off on her own and regroup.

This part of the farm gave her freedom. A place where she could stop thinking about things that bugged her. Out here it was simply about nature and horses. She reached the back paddock and climbed on the fence, smiling as a couple of the horses raised their heads to look at her, tails swishing lightly to keep the bugs away.

These were some of the forty horses they'd rescued from a horrific situation a few weeks ago. When Emily and her dad had found them, they'd been filthy, horribly thin, injured, and traumatized, locked in dark, windowless stalls, in mud up to their ankles.

And now . . . She grinned as she watched the horses lazing in the sun, their clean coats not exactly glistening, but hinting at new life and luster. She could still see their ribs, but there was a faint hint of padding over them now, even in such a short time.

Jaws raised his head to look at her and nickered softly. She'd named him Jaws to honor his courage when he'd tried to bite his old owner when the nasty man had tried to stop Emily and her dad from rescuing the horses.

Jaws been vicious for that one second, and ever since, he'd been nothing but happy and relaxed. He lazily lowered his head and began to graze again, his body so relaxed she could practically hear him humming with pleasure.

The best thing of all about the rescue was the spirit that was returning to the eyes of the horses they'd saved. They all seemed to sense they'd found safety, and she knew the eight they'd already sold had gone to good homes as well. There'd been forty originally, but they'd sold the ones that were in decent shape, so now they were down to thirty-two. Actually it was thirty-three, since Precious had given birth to T.J. after the mare had arrived at Running Horse Ridge.

Emily smiled at the thought of the baby colt her dad had given to her. T.J. was the first horse that she'd owned, and he was the cutest thing ever. She adored him and visited him every day . . . not that there was that much to do with him, since she couldn't ride him or really train him yet. Not like Sapphire.

She appreciated T.J.; she really did. But she still didn't understand why her dad had given her T.J. instead of Sapphire. He'd never given her an answer that made sense, not that anything he did anymore really made sense to her.

But now was about a little Shetland pony who needed a bath. Emily knew she'd feel better after taking care of him. She leaned on the railing of the paddock and searched the field for a small roan pony. She didn't remember rescuing him, but she'd been occupied with Precious most of the time, and she'd missed a lot of the action.

The grass was a little sparse in this paddock; the animals would have gotten sick if they'd been given too much rich grass all of a sudden. But the trees surrounding the paddock were tall, and the air was light and fresh. The blue sky was gorgeous, and the only sounds were the chirping of birds and the snorting of horses.

Emily looked out across the horizon and saw the rounded peak of Mount Saint Helens in the distance silhouetted against the blue sky. She still couldn't believe it was the same mountain as the photo in her aunt and uncle's den, with a pointed peak. Now the peak was curved, like the crown of someone's head, after the top half of the mountain had literally blown off when it had erupted in 1980.

Emily studied the mountain, trying to imagine what it would feel like to see thousands of tons of earth flying into the air straight at her. . . .

There was a loud snort, and she pulled her gaze back to the paddock. Hidden beneath the shadows of several large fir trees was a small cluster of horses . . . and there was a little tiny one hidden behind the rest, so small she could actually see his whole body beneath the belly of a tall Thoroughbred. She hopped down from the fence. "Found you."

She strolled over to the group of horses and patted a few noses and scratched a few whiskers, then peeked past the tall horse for her assignment.

He was gone.

Emily scanned the paddock, looking to the left in time to see a little shadow dart around the corner and out of sight.

She started after him. "You do realize that I'm here to give you treats, don't you?" she called out. "And I'm going to brush you and get all the snarls and mud out of your coat, and you'll feel wonderful." She rounded the corner and stopped abruptly at the sight of him.

The little pony was backed into a corner, his head up, his eyes wide, his nostrils flaring, as if she were some great enemy come to do him harm. His front feet were splayed, and his thick white mane almost completely covered his face. His mane spilled over all sides of his neck, nearly down to his chest. His coat, from what she could see beneath the mud, was a rich gold. A classic palomino and completely cute.

And apparently terrified of her.

Her heart tightened and she held out a carrot,

crooning softly. "Hey, little man, you're not at that awful place anymore. You're safe now. It's okay."

He backed up even farther, smashing himself in the corner and snorting loudly.

Emily kept talking quietly to him, holding out the carrot. "I know you're small, but I bet you're tough, aren't you? All ponies are. How about we name you Hercules, because you're so tough that there's nothing that can hurt you? Is that good? Should we call you Hercules?"

The tiny pony began to tremble, and she saw sweat begin to stain the hair on his neck, and her throat began to fill up. "You're that scared of me?"

His head wove back and forth, his eyes so wide she could see the white around the rims, and the skin on his flanks was vibrating, he was trembling so badly.

"Okay, so I won't touch you. How about I toss you the carrot?" Emily went down on her knees and tossed the carrot toward his feet.

The little pony's body jerked backward as she moved her hand, and he let out a panicked squeal and jumped sideways against the rails, pressing his whole body lengthwise along the split log rails, trapped in the corner by Emily.

She slowly lowered her hand, trying not to scare him

any further. "It's okay, Hercules. I'm not coming any closer. But there's food at your feet." Despite his thick coat, she could still see his hip bones sticking out and knew he was desperately skinny beneath his speckled coat, as were all the other horses they'd rescued. "It's a carrot." She pointed at it, and Hercules flinched.

She clenched her fists against the need to leap to her feet, rush over to him, and throw her arms around him. To hug him, to hold him, to make him realize that everything was all right and that he was safe now. But she knew she couldn't. That he wouldn't allow it.

Instead, she had to simply sit there and let him be terrified.

She cleared her throat and tried again. "My name is Emily. I'm from New Jersey. This farm belongs to my aunt and uncle, and I guess my dad, too. He inherited half of it when Grandpa died. They're nice here, especially to ponies like you. Everyone here loves you. Really, they do—"

He shuddered and she quickly stopped talking, feeling so utterly helpless to alleviate his terror.

She sat for another minute, watching the little pony flattened against the fence, his head up and turned through the rails away from her, his little body trembling, his neck thick with sweat. He made no indication he'd even seen the carrot, even though she was certain he must have smelled it. "Okay, how about I come back and visit later? Give you some space?"

She wiggled backward on the grass, not standing up until she was back around the corner and out of Hercules's sight.

Then she grabbed the fence rail and peered through it at the pony, barely able to see him across the distance, but pretty sure he wouldn't see her.

For a long moment he didn't move. Then he finally pulled his head out of the fence and turned to look where she'd been standing. When he didn't see her, he looked around the field carefully, then his little body expanded with a huge sigh and he dropped his head, his nostrils fluttering as the air blew out of his nose.

Then his ears went up, pointing straight at the carrot.

He lifted his head again and looked around the field, pausing to look in her direction. Emily froze, holding her breath.

Hercules pulled his gaze off her and he looked at the carrot, then he slowly took a step away from the fence, his movements cautious as he planted each tiny hoof carefully in the dirt.

He reached the carrot and swept it off the ground

with his teeth, munching eagerly, his tail giving a lazy swish of happy contentment as he ate it. His body wasn't trembling anymore, and he took his time inspecting the ground, snagging every single carrot remnant out of the dirt.

"Okay, Hercules," Emily said in a normal voice, not hiding when he snapped his head up and looked right at her. "I'll be back later with more carrots, now that I know you like them so much. We're going to be friends."

Hercules whirled away and galloped across the paddock to the other side, not stopping until he was clear across the field. Then he spun around and looked at her, his head held high, his body stiff.

Emily bit her lip, trying not to think about what had been done to him to make him so afraid of people . . . but she couldn't help it, and there were tears in her eyes when she turned away to head back to the barn.

She clenched her fists and jutted out her jaw. Somehow she was going to find a way to help Hercules.

Somehow.

It took Emily forty-five minutes to find Aunt Debby to tell her about Hercules and that was because Aunt Debby was in the one place Emily hadn't thought to look: in the stall of the only horse that actually belonged to Emily.

Emily frowned as she walked down the aisle and saw the open door in front of Precious and T.J.'s stall.

T.J. was a chestnut foal with a white crescent moon on his face. His red mane always stuck straight up, and his tail was so short it was barely as long as Emily's forearm. His legs were spindly, but he was running well already. Emily had spent time every day brushing both T.J. and Precious, and it was supposed to be *her* job: the one horse that she didn't have to ask Aunt Debby if she was allowed to touch.

And now Aunt Debby was taking over T.J. as well?

Emily couldn't help but scowl as she reached the stall and looked inside. Her dad and Aunt Debby were in the stall, huddled over T.J. "Um, hi."

Neither of them turned around. "Hey, Em." Her dad was stroking T.J.'s little mane and listening to Aunt Debby talk.

"What's going on?" Emily asked.

"We're checking on T.J.," her dad said.

Emily frowned. "Is something wrong with him?"

"No, we're doing some initial groundwork with him," her dad said.

Emily narrowed her eyes. "You're training him?"

"Sort of. In a way."

"But—" She set her hands on her hips and tried to keep herself calm. "But he's my horse. Aren't I supposed to be working with him? I thought you were going to coach me and I was going to do it?"

Her dad finally looked at her, his brow furrowed. He was wearing jeans and a pair of work boots, a T-shirt and a faded Red Sox hat. He hadn't even shaved! He was looking less and less like the suit-wearing businessman dad she'd had for twelve years and more and more like someone she didn't even know. "Em, it's important that T.J. be handled correctly from the start. We're just making sure—"

"Why don't you show me what needs to be done with him, and I can do it? How else am I supposed to learn?" She walked into the stall, peering past them at T.J. "At the very least, can't you tell me when you're working with him so I can watch and learn?" It would be so much fun to have something actually to *do* with T.J., since she couldn't ride him.

It was so difficult trying constantly to get Aunt Debby to give her more independence with the horses, and especially Sapphire, that T.J. had been her one relaxing moment of the day: when she knew no one would be looking over her shoulder questioning what she was doing with him. And now to find out that her dad and Aunt Debby had been training him on their own, without even bothering to *tell* Emily, let alone having her help . . . "He's my horse. I should be included."

Aunt Debby finally turned to look at her. She had that all-business expression on her face that Emily dreaded. "How's the pony?"

"Hercules?" Emily immediately forgot about being upset about T.J. "Oh, he's terrible." She quickly explained the situation with Hercules, knowing as she did that Aunt Debby would never let her be in charge of helping Hercules if she didn't even think Emily was capable of "doing some initial groundwork" with her own horse.

Aunt Debby sighed, her eyes sad. "That poor little guy."

Emily nodded. "You should have seen how badly he was shaking, and I wasn't even within twenty feet of him."

Aunt Debby looked at Emily's dad. "What do you think?"

Emily was so surprised, her mouth dropped open. Aunt Debby asking her dad for advice about horses? Her dad hadn't touched a horse in years before they'd arrived at the farm a few weeks ago, and Aunt Debby was a total control freak about the horses. And Aunt Debby trusted her dad's opinion? But not Emily's, even though Emily had been riding her whole life? Emily might not know *everything*, but she knew a lot. She'd heard her aunt asking Alison's opinion on horses, and Alison certainly didn't know more than Emily did.

What did she have to do to get Aunt Debby to take her as seriously as Emily wanted to be taken? It was so aggravating!

Emily's dad played with T.J.'s mane as Precious

happily munched her way through the hay. Her gray coat was already thicker and healthier than it had been when she first arrived, and there was a tiny layer of padding over her ribs now. "Sounds like Hercules needs time. Lots of it."

Aunt Debby nodded. "I agree. You have time?"

"Not that kind of time." Emily's dad sounded regretful. "Not with more than thirty extra horses that still need care."

Aunt Debby nodded. "I don't either." She looked at Emily. "See what you can do with him."

"Me?" Emily felt a sudden flash of pride and pulled her shoulders back. "Really?"

Aunt Debby nodded. "Just go and hang out with him. Talk to him. Be in his presence. Let him see that a person can be around him and not have to touch him. Once he lets you near him without getting upset, my schedule should have lightened up and I'll take over with actually socializing him. Maybe take a book out to the paddock and sit down and read."

Emily sagged. "So you just want me to stand near him and talk to him? To *read* in his presence? That's it? I can't even touch him?"

"Exactly. It will be wonderful for him. Your dad or I will take over the actual work with him once our schedules clear up, but it's important for Hercules to have human socialization until we're ready. Don't try to touch him. You could do more damage if you do it the wrong way."

"The wrong way?" Emily echoed, unable to keep the hurt out of her voice. "You don't trust me to be gentle with him?"

"No, no, no," Emily's dad said quickly. "You're wonderful with horses. But it sounds like Hercules needs a special touch."

Emily looked back and forth between her dad and her aunt and saw identical expressions on their faces, and she knew they didn't trust her. Not truly, not with something as important as Hercules or T.J. Or riding Sapphire. They trusted her with reading a book in the presence of a horse or giving baths to rescue horses, but not with anything that really mattered. "You do realize that I've been around horses my whole life, don't you? That I'm not a total idiot when it comes to horses?"

Aunt Debby raised her brows. "I don't think you're an idiot—"

"Kyle says you're going to have me ride in the Maiden class at the show, that it's a class for little kids. Is that right?"

"There will be some little kids in there, yes, but there

will also be some kids your age. Anyone who has just started riding will be in there, so it will be a good place to start." Aunt Debby patted T.J. one more time, then stood up. "There are a few more horses I want your opinion on, Scott, if you have a moment—"

"Wait!" Emily looked at her dad, desperate. "Dad, you know I don't belong in a beginner class with little kids. I've been riding my whole life, and I've won so many times—"

Her dad gave her an affectionate look. "This is different, Em. You're lucky you're eligible for the Maiden class. It'll be a great opportunity for you to build some confidence with jumping. You've done a lot of shows, but this will be a different experience."

"But—"

Her dad frowned at her, and then used a tone she'd never heard from him before: a tone that said he was the boss and she had to listen to him. "Emily, Aunt Debby knows what she's doing when it comes to horses. I would think you would understand that by now. I trust her instincts, and you should, too. You don't know as much as you think you do, and you're lucky to be on this farm to learn how to handle horses correctly. Okay?"

She stared at him, her heart shriveling. "Wow. You

sound like a real dad."

He smiled. "Is that a bad thing?"

"Yeah, maybe." She was horrified at how small her voice sounded, but she couldn't help it. "You know, you used to be my best friend."

Her dad stared at her for a moment, looking completely confused. "What?"

"Now you're Aunt Debby's." She tried to keep the tears out of her eyes. "Who cares? I don't need you anyway." She stalked out of the stall, blinking hard, ignoring both her aunt and her dad as they called out after her.

Why was it so difficult to fit in here? She was a rider, this was a barn . . . this was her world. Why wouldn't they trust her? Why were they forcing her to work so hard to prove herself?

All she knew is that she couldn't trust them to back her, to believe in her.

At her old barn everyone did. Here . . . She yanked open Sapphire's stall door and managed a teary smile when he whipped his head toward her and gave a soft whinny. "How do I make them believe in me, Sapphire?"

He perked his ears and gave her that same, adorable look he'd given her and Aunt Debby earlier. The look

Aunt Debby had said was perfect for the model class.

Emily lifted her chin. It was up to her, then. She had to be the one to trust herself and believe in herself. Be a star until she forced everyone else into treating her exactly the way she wanted to be treated. "You're right, Sapphire. We'll win. That's how I'll prove it. You and I will win the model class, I'll win the Maiden class on Moondance so I can't ride Maiden anymore, and I'll save Hercules." She did a little dance of victory as she imagined holding up that blue ribbon and waving it in her aunt's face. "We'll totally rock, they'll all be in awe, and they'll all want to kiss my toes."

Sapphire snorted and stomped his foot, and Emily held up her booted foot to his nose. "See this boot? Everyone will be trying to kiss it, and you're the only one who will be allowed."

He sniffed her foot, then opened his mouth to take a bite.

"Yikes!" She yanked her foot back. "Hey, beautiful, don't start taking advantage of how much I love you. There will be no toes on the menu today, okay?"

There was a snort from behind her and she turned around to find Max peering into the stall. "There's at least one old-timer here that likes me, huh, Max? You want to help me practice making Sapphire stand for the model class—" She froze as she had a sudden idea.

A brilliant one.

She did a quick dance of excitement, making both horses snort. She gave each horse a cheerful pat, knowing that she'd struck upon the perfect idea for making her toe-kissing plan a reality. "I'll be back in a little bit."

Then she shooed Max out of the stall, securely fastened the latch on Sapphire's door, and took off at a run, her feet light with excitement and anticipation.

*E*mily ran out the front door of the barn and found exactly who she was looking for: Meredith Jenkins, one of the girls who worked at the barn. She was Emily's age and had always been nice to her the few times they'd met. Definitely a potential ally.

In the gravel driveway of the barn Meredith was bathing a reddish chestnut horse with three white socks. His coat was wet, and he was nicely muscled and rounded out. Not a rescue horse, for sure. He was very cute, actually.

Instead of having him tied up in a nice wash stall with warm water as Emily would have done at home, Meredith had draped the lead shank over his neck while she sprayed his feet with a hose in the middle of the driveway. Every few seconds, he'd take a tiny step forward, and she'd order him to cut it out. And then he'd take another step, until she finally stopped, grabbed his lead shank and backed him up to where they'd started. Then she tossed the lead shank over his neck and squatted down to start scrubbing his white socks.

"Meredith!"

The girl glanced up and grinned when she saw Emily approach. "Hi, Emily. Congrats on getting Debby to let you near Sapphire again. Alison told me. Excellent work!"

Emily smiled back, glad she'd sought Meredith out. She didn't know her well, but she was the only person at the barn that Emily knew besides her own family. Meredith was occasionally invited to dinner, and she'd been at Family DVD Night last night, so Emily felt a little comfortable with her. Meredith had helped her out with Sapphire once, and ever since, they'd had a bit of a bond. "You want me to hold him?"

Meredith shot a warning look at the horse as he took another step. "No, he's fine. He's not going anywhere." She glared at the horse as he took another step, then got up, grabbed the lead shank and backed him up again. "Halo, stay here!"

"You getting him ready for his new owners?" Emily glanced down the driveway, half expecting to see a van from another barn rolling up to take the horse away. She dreaded those vans, knowing that in each one might be the people to see Sapphire and make a deal Aunt Debby couldn't turn down. "He looks ready to sell."

Meredith laughed. "No, I'm not selling him—as long as he's a good boy, that is." She tugged on the lead shank as Halo took another step. "Halo's mine."

"Yours?" Emily couldn't keep the surprise out of her voice. "But I thought all the horses here were part of the rescue-fix-and-resell deal."

"Most of them are." Meredith glanced at her watch. "But Debby also takes paying boarders to make money. I get free lessons in exchange for the work I do around here."

"Really?" Everyone at Emily's barn in New Jersey paid for lessons, and Emily was one of the few girls that helped out with chores. Emily did it because she liked to be there, not because she had to. Emily was the only one at her old barn who actually brushed her own horses, let alone did work for anyone else.

"Yep. But it's fun. I don't mind, and I learn so much working for Debby. She's brilliant, you know?"

Emily bit her lip. "You think?"

"Totally. I'm so lucky I was able to get in with her, because she doesn't take many new students." Meredith looked at her watch again, made a squeak of tension, and scooted down to Halo's back sock and started scrubbing that one. "But she's demanding, for sure. I have to get a horse ready for its new owners, who are arriving in less than an hour." She started scrubbing harder. "I'm so not going to have time to get everything ready by tomorrow."

"Tomorrow? You mean the horse show? You taking Halo?" Emily dumped some soap on her palms and started washing Halo's other back sock. The suds dripped down over his white hoof, making rivulets as they pooled around his foot. She smiled as the familiar scent of ivory soap drifted up to her nose, because that was the same type she used on Rhapsody back at home.

Meredith shot her a grateful look. "Thanks for the help. And yep, Halo and I are showing tomorrow. I'm so pumped."

"You riding in the Maiden class?" Emily tried to keep her voice casual.

Meredith laughed as Halo inched forward a couple steps. "Maiden? No way. I haven't been eligible for Maiden in years. We're doing the eleven to fourteen Opens and Large Pony."

"Large Pony? What's that?" Emily couldn't keep from grimacing at Meredith's reaction to the Maiden class. Would she think Emily was a loser for riding in Maiden?

"Large Pony is Hunter class, which means it's a class that judges the beauty of the pony. Large ponies have to measure between thirteen hands two inches and fourteen two. Medium ponies are twelve two to thirteen two, and small ponies are twelve two and under. The jumps are bigger for the larger ponies, obviously."

Emily thought about the big jumps Alison had been riding the other day, and then thought about the tiny ones that Aunt Debby had had her jump. "How big are large pony jumps?"

"Three feet." Meredith scooted over to where Halo now stood, so she could keep scrubbing his sock.

"Three feet? Seriously?" The jumps Emily had done couldn't have been even half that. How cool would that be to jump three feet? "What's Maiden?"

Meredith frowned. "I don't know. Maybe eighteen inches."

Eighteen inches? Yikes. Moondance would be able to step over those at a walk. Emily was pretty sure that she'd jumped higher than that in both her lessons. She moved over to where Halo had moved, and started scrubbing his sock again. "What kind of class is Open eleven to fourteen?"

"Equitation. Judges the form of the rider. Once you get in the Open division, it's divided into age groups. I'm twelve, so I ride in the eleven through fourteen classes."

Equitation. That would be what Emily should excel at. Her form was brilliant, after years of coaching by Les. "Is Maiden hunter or equitation?"

"Equitation. An over-fences class and a flat class."

Emily relaxed a little. She should have no trouble winning an equitation class filled with beginners, especially on the flat! Easy-peasy! She wiggled her toes inside her paddock boots, pleased that the toe-kissing plan was going so well. "Can I ask you something?"

"Sure." Meredith grabbed the hose and pointed it at Halo's sock and squeegeed the soap out with her hand until his pink skin glowed underneath the white hair. She pointed the hose toward the sock Emily had been scrubbing. "Done?"

"Yep." Emily rubbed her fingers through Halo's hair as Meredith sprayed the sock with the hose, the water cold on Emily's hands. Halo took a step, and they both laughed and moved over with him. "Do you know much about the model classes?"

"Sure do. The first Large Pony class has that element. The top ponies after the jumping class are brought back for conformation judging before final placement." Meredith tossed Emily a towel, and they both squatted and began to dry Halo's legs.

"Aunt Debby wants me to show Sapphire in a model class tomorrow. Will you give me some tips?"

Meredith shot her a wide grin. "Oh, totally! That will be so fun! I'm going to practice with Halo later today. We'll do it together, okay?"

Emily beamed at Meredith, unable to stem her excitement. "That would be fantastic. I want to do well with him."

Meredith peered at her under Halo's brown belly, which was still dripping with water. "I got to show Sapphire once when he first arrived. Debby wanted to see how he did."

Emily felt a tinge of jealousy. "You did? How was it?"

Meredith grinned. "It was *awesome*."

"Ooh," Emily sighed. "I bet it was."

"I only did a flat class—no jumps—but everyone was watching, wanting to know who this beautiful horse was."

The towel slipped out of Emily's fingers as she leaned

forward to listen. "Really? Was he good?"

Meredith snorted. "He was terrible. Took off and ran over the judge."

Emily laughed and picked up her towel again. "I can totally see him doing that! I bet he looked good doing it, though."

"Of course he did. Sapphire looks good all the time." Meredith caught Halo's lead shank as her horse took a few more steps. "And he knows it, too."

Emily giggled. "He does, doesn't he? He thinks he can get away with anything because he's beautiful."

"Totally!" Meredith jumped to her feet, her cheeks flushed. "I was so honored when he took off with me on him. I love his spirit."

"Me too!" Emily leaped up as well. "I thought I was the only one! Aunt Debby wants to crush his spirit!"

Meredith shook her head as Halo took a small walk around them. "No she doesn't. She just wants to manage it enough to make him the star he can be."

Emily wrinkled her nose. "She has high hopes for him, doesn't she?"

"Oh, yes. He's the golden horse of the barn, for sure."

"Believe me, I know. She's so possessive of him." Emily cocked her head, thinking about Meredith and

Sapphire running over the judge. "Did she bust you when he was bad at the show?"

"Me? Not at all. It wasn't my fault."

Emily frowned. "How do you get to that point? Getting Aunt Debby to have that kind of faith in you? To have her not blame you for things that go wrong around you?" She knew for sure that if she allowed Sapphire to run down the judge tomorrow, Aunt Debby would use it as an excuse to limit Emily's freedom with him.

Meredith got a sympathetic look on her face. "Don't worry, Emily. Debby didn't trust me at first, either. She watched me all the time and was always checking up on everything I did."

"Really?" Emily searched Meredith's face to see if she was telling the truth. "She did?"

"Yep. But eventually she realized that I was smart enough to know what I could and couldn't do, and she backed off. You'll get there. And we'll start by making Sapphire do really well in the class tomorrow. You'll show her."

Emily grinned. "I will, won't I?"

"Of course you will." Meredith glanced at her watch. "But it'll have to be later. I have to run." She started tugging Halo toward the barn. "Let's hook up later to practice for the model class! Four o'clock, okay?" She hustled Halo into the barn, his feet clopping on the floor as he trotted after her.

"Yeah, four works." Emily gazed after the pair, suddenly wishing so badly that she could have her own horse the way Meredith did. Really having her own horse. Not like T.J., who was hers only as long as it was convenient for her aunt and her dad. It wasn't as if Emily actually had any independence with T.J. Clearly her aunt didn't trust her ability to make smart choices, like how Meredith had described. Plus, it wasn't like Emily could show T.J. and ride him. Emily wanted a horse to ride and take care of with no one looking over her shoulder to make sure she was doing everything right.

Then Meredith glanced back over her shoulder and gave Emily a thumbs-up before disappearing around the corner.

Excitement rushed through Emily. If Meredith could have Sapphire plow down a judge and not get blamed for it, there was hope for Emily. Tomorrow she would prove it. Tomorrow would rock! Wait until Aunt Debby saw her and Sapphire . . .

There was going to be no judge-trampling tomorrow. No way.

*E*mily! You're not paying attention."

"Sorry, Meredith." Emily winced, trying to put Hercules out of her mind and concentrate on making Sapphire stand correctly. She'd run up to the paddock to see Hercules again before meeting Meredith to train, and he'd been just as scared of her as he had been earlier.

She couldn't stop thinking of the terror in his little brown eyes, and she felt so bad.

"Okay, so walk and come to a stop again," Meredith ordered. "Like you're lining up in front of the judge."

Emily grabbed Sapphire's reins, and walked him forward a few steps.

She lifted his head and eased him to a stop, and his front feet stopped in perfect alignment. She did a quick check of his back feet and saw one foot was stretched out behind him too far, so she pulled him forward another step and all his feet lined up correctly.

"Nice," Meredith said as she strolled up to Sapphire, pretending she was a judge inspecting him, letting Halo trail behind her. "His ears?"

Emily pulled a piece of wax paper out of her pocket and crinkled it under Sapphire's nose. His ears popped forward to inspect it, and his eyes were all alert—then his lip popped out and he swept the wax paper out of Emily's hand and started to chew it.

Meredith groaned as Emily grabbed the paper and tried to pry it from his teeth. "He can't do that in the class," Meredith said.

"I know." A piece of paper ripped free in Emily's hand, and the rest disappeared into his mouth. "I won't let him get it next time." Emily gave up on the wax paper and scowled at him as he spit it onto the driveway. "Nice, Sapphire. Really attractive."

He lowered his head and nuzzled against her hip, and she immediately hugged him. "Okay, you're forgiven."

But Meredith had her hands on her hips, her face all serious. "Emily, you can't let him nudge you in the class, either. He has to simply stand there and look beautiful."

"I know." Emily released him, trying to give him a stern look. "You be good, you hear me?"

He snorted and gave her a shove that nearly knocked her off her feet.

Meredith cocked her head. "You know, there's a reason why Debby makes him behave around the barn. Because if he messes around in a class—"

"I'll be careful in the class." Emily scratched his ears, chuckling at his moan of delight. "He'll be perfect." But he gave her a slight nudge to knock her off balance, and she felt a little flash of wariness. What if he wasn't good? What if he *did* trample the judge?

She studied him carefully, looking him in the eye. Sapphire loved her, and she needed him to be good. They'd be fine. She grimaced and hoped she was right.

"This is what you need to do." Meredith grabbed Halo's reins tighter and turned him away. "Watch."

She walked Halo across the driveway, then turned and clucked him into a trot. He stretched out his neck, showing a beautiful arc, and he pointed his toes as he trotted, gliding across the gravel like a ballet dancer. His ears were forward, his muscles gliding under his shiny coat.

Then Meredith eased him to a walk in a graceful transition; finally she circled him around and halted him. His front feet stopped in perfect alignment; one back foot was forward under his belly and the other was placed at the exact right spot slightly back. She moved her hand by her hip and Halo's ears perked forward, his nose extended to show off his muscled neck and his beautiful head.

He kept the position for several moments until she patted his neck and grinned at Emily. "And that, my friend, is how it's done."

Sapphire chose that moment to give Emily a hard shove, and she landed on her butt in the gravel. Emily glared up at him, feeling the first true worries that maybe her toe-kissing plan might be a little harder to accomplish than she'd thought. "And that, my darling horse, is *not*."

*I*t was after nine that night and the sun was down, when Emily finally settled in to braid Sapphire. She'd been tied up in a family dinner for almost an hour, and then Caitlyn had insisted on showing Emily her ribbons, including her ribbon from her Maiden win, which she'd framed and put over her bed. Kyle had been with them, and he'd been making fun of Emily, but Caitlyn was so cute and so excited about Emily getting to ride Maiden, that Emily had actually felt better.

Caitlyn might be seven, but her total excitement that Emily was in their life was such a great ego boost. After hanging with Caitlyn, Emily had skipped the whole way to the barn to get Sapphire, still chuckling at Caitlyn's protests when Aunt Debby had said it was too late for Caitlyn to go to the barn and hang out with Emily. At least there was one person at the barn under more restrictions than Emily!

And now Sapphire was cross-tied in his stall, and she had filched a step stool from the supply room. Despite Sapphire's aversion to being cross-tied, Emily had been forced to do it, because it was impossible to braid a squirmy horse, and Sapphire was the king of squirmy.

She'd given him a carrot and apologized, and he'd seemed to forgive her. And now the barn was quiet except for the contented sounds of horses bedding down for the night. The fresh scents of hay and pine shavings wrapped around Emily, making her feel cozy and warm. There was no one around at all, making Emily feel like she owned the place. She could almost pretend she was the boss and no one would tell her what to do.

She used her comb to part a three-quarter-inch section of Sapphire's mane, and glanced out at the aisle again. The empty aisle. All hers. Her rules!

Sapphire snorted and she jumped at the sudden noise, losing her grip on the braid. She turned around to laugh at herself with someone, then remembered that she was there alone.

Yeah. Alone.

Emily realized that she loved the privacy, but in her old barn, it never took long before her friends showed up to braid their own horses. That was when they all owned the barn together. Played music. Told jokes. Planned for the next day.

Emily sighed and slid the pulling comb through Sapphire's mane to separate another small section to braid. She missed her friends. Even Jenny Smith, who she hated half the time. Missed belonging . . .

There was a thud from the aisle, and Emily peered toward the sound. "Hello?"

Meredith marched by Sapphire's stall. "I can't believe you're in here alone!" Meredith plunked an iPod player with speakers on a hay bale. "You can't braid by yourself! Too boring!" She hit play, and the high-energy beat of the Xtremes echoed through the barn. "Now, that's fun!"

Meredith threw up her arms and started dancing; happiness swelled in Emily's chest. "Took you long enough to get here," she teased Meredith, *so happy* to have company.

Emily began singing along with the music, laughing at Meredith's horrible dancing. Sapphire threw up his head and swished his tail, and Emily grinned. "Sapphire's dancing, too."

"Of course he is. The boy has good taste." Meredith held up her finger. "Don't stop singing. I'll be right back."

Emily leaned around the stall door, watching as Meredith ran off, unable to contain her glee. Now *this* was what the night before a show was supposed to be like!

She was still tapping her foot when Meredith reappeared, leading Halo, and carrying a feed bucket and some braiding supplies. Meredith started singing again as she hooked Halo up to the aisle cross ties outside Sapphire's stall, then she hopped up on an inverted white bucket so she could see what she was doing with the braids. She held up dark green, navy, and black yarn. "What color?"

There were choices? Emily had done black because she always wore black for dressage. "What color is your jacket?"

"I have all colors." Meredith studied the yarn. "I think I'll go with my green jacket and beige breeches tomorrow. This green's a little slanted toward the hunter side, but that's okay." She tossed the other two skeins over her shoulder without even looking where they were landing, and Emily laughed as one of them landed in a water bucket with a splash.

Meredith giggled. "Oops." She began looping the yarn around her elbow and hand to cut a bunch of pieces to the correct length, and she wandered over to Sapphire as she did it. "Can I see?"

"Sure." Emily jumped off the stool she'd used and stepped aside, suddenly getting a little nervous. What if her braids weren't good enough?

Meredith climbed on the step stool and peered at the braids, then let out a low whistle. "I can't wait to see Debby's face when she sees these."

"Really? Are they bad?"

Meredith hopped down. "I don't think I've ever seen so many braids."

"That's good, right?"

"It's incredible. Those braids are so tight and even. Want to do Halo's? I'll pay you twenty bucks and be your friend?"

Emily smiled and relaxed as she climbed back up. "No, thanks. I still have to do Moondance after this."

"Moondance? You showing her?" Meredith cut the yarn and then draped the bunch over Halo's withers.

"Yep." Emily decided not to mention it was in the Maiden class, and instead focused on sliding her metal pulling comb through Sapphire's mane, making a perfect part about three quarters of an inch down from the last braid. She stuck the comb in her back pocket, divided the hair into three even segments, then began to braid, pulling the hair as tightly as she could. When she was about halfway down, she started to weave the black yarn into the braid.

"Maiden?" Meredith asked.

Emily grimaced. "Yeah."

Meredith nodded. "You'll win, no problem."

Emily's embarrassment faded at the total confidence in Meredith's voice. "You think?"

"Absolutely. You—"

"Hi, guys." Alison walked down the aisle, leading a gorgeous gray horse covered in dapples. The tips of his ears and his nose were dark gray. His mane and tail were black with specks of white, and his coat was this awesome mixture of coal gray and bright white dapples.

For a gray horse to be that dark, the horse had to be quite young, because the older they got, the more white they turned. Like Max, who was almost pure white now.

Emily had never seen the horse before and she knew instantly that he was an expensive animal. "Who's that?"

Alison hooked the horse up to aisle cross ties so

he was facing Halo. "He's my new horse. His show name's Black Ice, and I'm calling him Icy. He arrived yesterday."

"Wow." Meredith let out a sigh of appreciation. "He's gorgeous."

"Yours?" Emily frowned. "As in yours to train for resale?"

"Nope." Alison climbed up on a step stool and began to comb through Icy's mane. "He's mine. We sold my old horse during the winter, and we've been looking for a replacement ever since. We wanted a young one with lots of potential, and we finally found him a couple weeks ago. Isn't he fantastic? You should see him jump. He can trot four-foot oxers." She looked so very pleased. "He's got springs for legs."

Emily felt more than a pang of jealousy as Alison began to braid Icy's mane. Both Meredith and Alison had their own horses? Beautiful horses they could train and take to shows and compete on? And Emily was stuck riding school horses and hoping for Aunt Debby to grant her a chance to show them. In New Jersey *she* was the one who had the great horse and did all the shows. She liked being *that* girl a lot better!

"Good song." Alison began to wiggle in place on her step stool as another Xtremes song came on the player.

"This group kicks. I downloaded a few of their tracks onto my playlist. I've been dying to hear this one."

Meredith started snapping her fingers and throwing her hips side to side. "You're showing Icy tomorrow?"

"I don't know yet. At the moment the plan is to ride him around the show grounds and see how he reacts to all the craziness. We might try a class or two if he seems to be adjusting, so we can get an idea of where he is. We'll play it by ear." Alison started to sing along to the song then stopped. "Oh, I forgot. I ordered pizza for us. Should be here in about a half hour. Hope you all didn't eat too much at dinner."

Pizza? Emily's stomach started to grumble at the thought of it, despite the burger she'd eaten not so long ago. There was just something about pizza at night that was so delicious. "Thanks for doing that, Alison." She felt a little shy speaking up, still intimidated by her cousin, even though she was only one year older than Emily. They'd started to break through the ice, but Emily still felt a little insecure around her, especially now that she knew Alison had her own horse. A gorgeous horse that trotted four-foot oxers. Oxers were jumps that had a front rail and a back rail, making the jump wide as well as high, which meant it was a *big* jump.

Alison gave her the thumbs-up. "Barn tradition.

Pizza for the braiders the night before the show. On my mom."

A new song came on the player, and Emily grinned as Alison and Meredith let out simultaneous squeals. "I love this song!"

Both of them started to sing at the top of their lungs while they braided, and after a minute, Emily joined in. The beat of the drums thudded in her belly, Alison's feet were stomping in rhythm on her wooden step stool, and even Sapphire was shaking his head.

Emily chuckled as she tied another braid, still shouting out the song as she watched Alison and Meredith dancing in the aisle, their fingers flying over the braids.

She hadn't realized how *much* she missed her friends at her old barn, how much she missed the camaraderie. She wouldn't call Alison a friend yet, but Meredith was getting there. . . .

"Oh, and Emily?"

Emily looked at Alison. "Yes?"

"Mom figured you didn't have the right clothes for riding in a hunter/jumper show, so you can go through my closet and pick out some of my old stuff to wear."

"Oh, me too," Meredith said. "I was just getting rid of some of my stuff, so I can bring that in the morning, too."

Emily blinked in surprise at their offer, glad she didn't have to accept wearing someone else's stuff that was so old that even they weren't wearing it anymore. There was something about hand-me-downs that made riding a borrowed horse in beginner class even more humiliating. She needed to be in power mode tomorrow, not hand-me-down mode. "Thanks, but I have nice stuff of my own. . . ." Her words faded as she realized she hadn't brought any of her show stuff with her from New Jersey, anyway. With the show in the morning, she didn't have time to get it. What had she been thinking? She hadn't even *thought* about show clothes!

Alison raised her brows. "You can't wear that funky dressage stuff in the show tomorrow. You'll look . . . odd. It would make the barn look like we don't know what we're doing, and Mom would never go for that. Really, I don't mind. Come up to my room later, and we can go through and find something that will fit you okay."

And just like that, the night stopped being quite so fun.

It was almost midnight by the time Emily got back to her room with her borrowed hand-me-downs for the show. She folded her arms and studied the assortment of riding clothes on her bed, trying to think of something positive about the situation. *Anything* positive. "Well, at least no one will mistake me for an arrogant, rich snob."

She snorted at herself. Yeah. Three cheers for that.

There were two jackets and three pairs of breeches from Alison. All of them were faded and worn, and none of them fit Emily quite right. She sighed with longing, thinking of the beautiful clothes she had for dressage shows, how perfect she was accustomed to looking. She thought of what her coach, Les, would say if he saw her enter the ring wearing clothes that looked like hand-me-downs. He'd say she shouldn't even bother to compete, because the image she presented when she entered the ring would doom her.

Emily bit her lip and thought of beautiful Sapphire. His braids looked fantastic, probably the best braid job she'd ever done. Even Moondance's had been pretty good, even though she'd been so tired by then.

But even Moondance's were worthy of a rider who didn't look frumpy. And Sapphire . . . she so wouldn't be worthy of standing in his shadow.

Oy. She was going to be Frumpy Girl tomorrow.

There was nothing inspiring about being Frumpy Girl. Frumpy Girl would come in last. No one would kiss the toes of Frumpy Girl.

She scratched her collarbone and tried to figure out what she could do to ditch the Frumpy Girl mind-set and become Winner Girl instead. . . .

The door was suddenly flung open, and Emily turned to see her younger cousin Caitlyn. Caitlyn's eyes were sparkling, and she was wearing a pink nightgown with a pinto horse on the front. "Emily!"

Emily smiled at her little cousin. "What's up?"

"I can't go to the show tomorrow because I'm going

to my friend Tanya's birthday party, so I wanted to wish you good luck!" Caitlyn then threw herself at Emily and gave her a giant hug that nearly knocked Emily over.

Emily laughed and peeled Caitlyn off her, feeling better. "Thanks. I appreciate it."

"You'll do awesome—" Caitlyn stopped and cocked her head, and they heard Aunt Debby calling for her. "Oops. Gotta go to bed. Bye!" She raced out, slamming the door shut behind her, leaving Emily chuckling.

Well, maybe seven-year-old girls would kiss the toes of Frumpy Girl.

There was a light tap at the door. "Em?"

She stiffened at her dad's voice. "What?"

"Can I come in?"

She sighed, trying to pretend she wasn't still upset by his treatment of her this afternoon. "Whatever."

The door opened, and her dad peered in. His light brown hair was tousled, longer than she'd ever seen it before, and he *still* hadn't shaved. But his blue eyes were bright, almost glowing, an expression she realized she hadn't seen ever before. He looked . . . alive. Yeah, that was it. He'd never been truly alive before they'd come back to the farm? The way he looked made her feel good.

"Hi, Em." He smiled at her. He looked happy. Truly happy.

"How come I never made you this happy?" The words tumbled out before she could stop them, and she felt bad when the happiness fell off his face.

"What are you talking about?"

"You." She turned away from him and began gathering the borrowed clothes off the bed. "You look happy. Weren't you ever happy when it was only the two of us? I wasn't enough for you?"

"Em!" Her dad's hand fell on her shoulder and he caught her wrist with the other, stopping her efforts to shrug him off. "Look at me."

She bit her lip and looked up at him, at the face of the person who'd been her only family her whole life until they'd popped into the farm a few weeks ago and she'd met family that were strangers. *His* family. "What?"

"You make me happy, sweetie. You always have." He held up his finger when she started to talk. "But it's a nice feeling to be back with my family again, to be on the farm where I grew up. But it's only a nice feeling because you're here with me." He cupped her chin. "Do you understand? Without you, I'd hate it here. You're my number one, hon, and you always will be."

Emily's eyes filled up. "Then why won't you stand up to Aunt Debby and tell her how great I am? That she can trust me?"

"Aw, Em." Her dad sat down on the bed. "It's different out here. The horses are the livelihood of this ranch. They come first."

She didn't sit down. "And I'll hurt them?"

He looked at her, and she saw a firmness in his gaze she'd never seen. "Emily, riding Rhapsody in a dressage class is not the same thing as dealing with abused and neglected horses or jumping even a well-trained horse. It takes time to build those skills, and I feel that Aunt Debby is a more unbiased judge of your readiness than I am, so I defer to her. If it were up to me, I'd let you ride any horse you want in any class you want, and I'm not sure that would be the best thing for you."

She narrowed her eyes, steeling herself against his words. She couldn't let herself believe it. "So at the show tomorrow, you won't stand up for me? What if I do well in the Maiden class? Then will you tell Aunt Debby she should enter me in another class?"

"I'm not going to the show."

She stared at him, too stunned to know what to say. Her dad had never missed a show. *Ever.*

"I need to stay at the farm and take care of the horses.

There are too many at-risk animals here right now, and both Aunt Debby and I can't be away."

"But—"

He smiled, but there was an element of sadness in his gaze. "Trust me, Emily, I wish I could go. But you'll be okay without me, and the horses need me more than you do."

"No, they don't! I need you! You're my *dad*!"

"I'll always be your dad, Em, but you're a big girl now, and you'll have Aunt Debby there."

"She hates me!"

His smile faded. "Now, Emily, I've had enough of you saying bad things about Aunt Debby. She doesn't hate you; she's a good person and an excellent horsewoman and you need to trust her judgment as I do."

She blinked hard at the tears rising in her eyes and clenched her fists against the urge to cry, to beg him to be the way he used to be.

"But I brought you something." He got off the bed and walked out into the hall, then came back with a dress bag. "For you."

She frowned, trying to shift thoughts. "What is this?"

"Open it."

She set the garment bag on the bed and unzipped

it, then gasped when she saw a brand-new, navy riding jacket and a pair of rust breeches with suede knee pads and the tag still on. And a crisp, white long-sleeved shirt with a choker collar. "Dad!"

He reached behind the door again, then tossed her a hatbox. "I knew you didn't have any clothes for the show, so I stopped in town and picked up some things for you. I called the tack store in New Jersey to find out your sizes, so I hope they work."

Emily ripped the box open and held up a black helmet, the velvet intact and beautiful. "It's incredible!" She tossed it on the bed and threw herself at him, burying her face in his chest while his arms wrapped around her and hugged her tight. "Thank you so much."

He chuckled and kissed the top of her head. "It's to make up for the fact I'm not going tomorrow. Forgiven?"

She grinned up at him. "No."

He ruffled her hair, and got a more serious look on his face. "There's one more thing."

"What?"

He dug into his back pocket and pulled out a little box wrapped in newspaper. "For you."

It was her dad's typical wrapping job, and seeing the crooked newsprint made her feel better. More secure.

Maybe her dad was changing, but he was still her dad in the little ways.

She sat down on the bed and carefully opened it as the mattress shifted when her dad sat next to her.

It was a small white jewelry box, and when she lifted the lid, she saw a silver choker pin for her riding shirt. It was a profile of a horse's head set inside a horseshoe. The horse was braided and tacked up, clearly ready for a show. The silver was polished and shiny, but there were scratches on it, and the edges were worn.

"That was your mom's choker pin." Her dad's voice was gruff.

"Mom's?" He'd never given her anything belonging to her mom before, not even a photo. She'd died when Emily was two, so Emily didn't remember her, and her dad never talked much about her . . . until now. "She rode horses?"

"Yep." Her dad carefully took the pin out of the box and flipped it over. "I gave this to her for her sixteenth birthday. Before we'd even started dating. We were just friends back then."

Emily saw an engraving on the back, and she took the pin and held it to the light by the bed to read it. "To O. Love, S."

Olivia. Her mom. Scott. Her dad.

"She wore it for every show, and when we moved away, she wore it on the lapel of her jackets when we went out for dinner." He brushed his finger over it. "I kept it for a long time, and now it's your turn to have it. She'd want you to wear it." He cleared his throat and stood up. "Now, it's off to bed. You have an early rise tomorrow, kiddo."

Emily bunched her fist around the pin and looked up. "Thanks, Dad."

He chucked her lightly on her shoulder. "You'll do great tomorrow."

"I wish you were going."

Regret flickered across his face. "So do I, hon. Maybe next time."

"*Maybe?* This isn't the only one you're going to miss?"

"I don't know. We'll see." He pecked her cheek, then slipped out of the room before she could protest even more.

But she'd seen the guilt on his face, and she knew the answer.

The pin and the clothes . . . they were guilt gifts, like she'd seen her friends at her old barn get all the time from their parents who were too busy to bother with the kids. But not her dad. He'd always been there. *Always.*

And now he was giving her guilt gifts instead.

She looked down at the pin in her hand and grinned.

But they were really, really good ones.

*E*mily's eyes snapped open, and she looked at the clock by her bed. Three thirty-five in the morning. Ten minutes before her alarm was supposed to go off.

Ten more minutes to sleep? Never!

She kicked off her covers and jumped to her feet, her heart pounding with excitement as she looked out the window. The lights were on in the barn already, and horses were calling for their breakfast.

The big horse van was pulled up next to the barn, headlights on, the growl of the engine so loud in the silence of early morning. She closed her eyes and let the sound of the motor rumble through her, the deep rattle that could be nothing but a horse van on the morning of the show, ready to take them off to another fantastic day.

She squealed and hugged herself, then grabbed her robe and sprinted for the bathroom.

Eight minutes later, Emily ran into the barn, her garment bag over her shoulder and a duffel bag with her boots and other gear in her hand. She'd put her chaps on over her new breeches to keep them clean and was wearing paddock boots so her freshly polished tall boots wouldn't get scuffed.

Uncle Rick was there already, filling hay nets with hay for the trip, and Aunt Debby was making the rounds with grain for the horses that were going. The lights in the barn cast a warm glow against the darkness of the night that was still hovering.

There were the fresh scents of hay, of clean shavings, and fresh water, and everything was perfect. "Hi!"

Uncle Rick glanced up. "You can toss your stuff in the head of the van. Then go wrap Sapphire and Moondance and get them ready to go. Bell boots for both of them to protect their front feet."

"Of course!" Emily ran to the van, grabbed a hand-hold, and wedged her foot on the front tire, then hauled herself up the four feet to the head. There was already a stack of hay bales lodged inside, along with six red water buckets and a number of fully stocked brush buckets that she guessed simply stayed in the van for horse shows—and suddenly she knew the day was going to be great.

This might be a hunter/jumper show with different rules and clothes and a different coach, but it was still a horse show, and this was her territory. This is what she loved.

It didn't matter if she was showing in Maiden or that she wasn't allowed to ride Sapphire. There was magic in the air, and great things were going to happen today, for sure!

She hummed happily as she hung up the garment bag with her new jacket, then tucked her duffel beneath it as she'd done so many times in the past. Then she brushed her fingers over her new choker pin as she turned back to the door of the van and thought of her mom. Had she started in Maiden, too?

Emily giggled as she swung down out of the van and headed toward Sapphire's stall to wrap his legs for the van ride. She was willing to bet that her mom had also started in Maiden if she'd been riding at Running Horse Ridge at the time.

Sapphire stuck his head over the door and whickered

when he saw her coming.

"Hiya, beautiful." She patted his nose and peeked at his braids, hoping he hadn't rubbed them out during the night. Some horses had to be braided on the morning of the show, because they would rub their braids right out during the night, and you never knew what kind of horse you had until that first time you braided him.

Emily stood on her tiptoes and inspected her braids. Still tight.

She grinned and knew then that everything was going to be all right. Better than all right. It was going to be *perfect*.

Emily perched on the bed in the back of the horse van's cab, peering out the windshield as they pulled into the show grounds. Aunt Debby was driving, Alison was riding shotgun, and Emily was in the back with Meredith.

Meredith's parents were coming later, but she'd needed a ride to the show, so she'd squeezed in with them.

The sun was bright and shining as they turned into a dirt driveway that led into a massive field. It was so massive she couldn't see the other side of it. It was more like a fairground in the middle of the woods than a field.

They were almost two hours late due to an accident on the highway, and Aunt Debby was stressing because they'd all missed the preshow warm-up that had run from six thirty to eight thirty. It was, apparently, a chance to jump the courses in an unjudged warm-up, and Emily was seriously wishing that she'd had the chance to practice before tackling the course in the Maiden class. Les was totally into being prepared, and it would have been nice to get in some more practice.

Not that she could do anything about it, right? No point in freaking.

Aunt Debby turned the van off the dirt road and began to bump over the grass toward the other vans. There were two rings off to the left with jumps. Instead of fences, they were marked with white stakes and orange tape strung between them, clearly no more than temporary rings in a field that was empty when there was no horse show going on.

The place was packed with vans and people and dogs and horses. Emily had missed this energy so much! "This is *awesome*."

The announcer's voice echoed over the fields, and Emily could hear him announcing the start of the Large Pony Hunters and the Maiden— "Maiden!" She sat up. "It's starting now?"

"Yep. The flat class is first on the list here. Meredith, your class is up first, too," Aunt Debby said. "Start getting ready now, girls. It's going to be tight."

Emily immediately started unzipping her chaps, wishing she'd kept her gear bag in the cab with her. Her heart was pounding, adrenaline kicking in as she quickly untied her paddock boots. She nearly tipped over when the van lurched over a rut in the field.

"I'll get Halo," Alison announced as Meredith calmly pulled out her jacket and began to put it on.

"I'll get the numbers and meet you guys at the ring," Aunt Debby said.

Emily glanced around as the van lumbered to a stop and realized there was no one left to help her with Moondance. Yikes! She was on her own! The van doors flew open, and everyone jumped out. Aunt Debby took off at a run across the fields while Alison yanked the ramp out of the van.

Emily bolted across the grass and hauled herself up into the head, where Meredith was already getting her tack.

Meredith tucked her hair under her helmet. "Good luck, and have fun. You'll totally dominate."

Emily shoved her hair into a ponytail and threw on a hairnet, then squashed her helmet onto her head.

"Yeah, good luck, too."

"Oh, it'll be fun." Now ready, since she'd had her stuff in the cab of the van with her, Meredith grabbed her tack and a brush box and climbed down, leaving Emily behind to get her boots on, find her jacket and gloves, and get her tack.

"Ack!" She was never going to make it!

She hadn't even gotten her boots on when Alison hollered from outside. "Emily! Toss me your saddle and bridle. I'll tack up Moondance for you!"

"Really?" Gasping with relief, Emily grabbed her saddle and bridle and ran to the door. Alison was standing below, arms up, holding on to Moondance's lead shank. Meredith was just disappearing between two vans, trotting Halo briskly along the grass. "Thanks!"

Alison nodded. "No problem. Team effort at shows." She grabbed Emily's tack and threw the saddle over Moondance's back. "Hurry up, though."

"Right." Emily raced back to her gear, hooked the boot pulls over the tabs, and yanked on her second boot. She slammed her heel into the floor to get it all the way on. "Come on!" Having boots that fit like a glove was great once they were on and looking good, but getting them on in a rush . . . not so good.

The leather finally slid over her calf, and she wrenched

the boot pulls out, grabbed her jacket and gloves, and leaped down. Alison was just tightening Moondance's noseband as Emily buttoned her jacket. "Leg up?"

"Yeah, thanks." Emily bent her left leg at the knee and Alison hooked her fingers below Emily's knee.

"On three," Alison said. "One, two, three."

Emily leaped on "three," and Alison easily tossed her on Moondance's back. "Okay, so you're going to the ring closest to us." Alison checked Moondance's girth, then tightened it another notch while Emily adjusted her jacket. "My mom will meet you outside the gate with your number. Then your class with Sapphire will be right after, so ride Moondance straight over to the other ring, and I'll meet you there with him."

Emily nodded. "You'll get him ready?"

"Yep." Alison patted her knee. "Now, go!"

Go. Emily grabbed Moondance's reins and spun the horse toward the ring, nudging the big gray mare into a trot while Emily frantically tried to organize her grip on the reins. Moondance's head was up, and her tail was frisky, swishing around with excitement as they rode past numerous vans and horses, blankets flapping, dogs racing around, everyone shouting and laughing and getting ready.

Moondance shied to the left as a girl came running

down a ramp just as they were passing a van, and Emily nearly lost her seat in the move. "Okay, girl, calm down." Emily patted the mare's neck as she looked ahead and saw a bunch of horses entering the ring closest to her. Her class was starting without her! "Shoot!"

She kicked Moondance into a canter, and winced at the sound of Les's voice in her mind screaming at her for not doing a proper warm-up. As if she had time! Moondance's gait was lumbering and bouncing on the grass, especially since she wasn't at all balanced, and Emily rose into a half-seat, perching above the saddle to make the canter more comfortable. She'd have to sit at the canter once the class started, but for now—

"Emily!"

Emily hauled Moondance to a stop as Aunt Debby raced toward her waving a white cardboard number. "Here!" She tossed it up at Emily. "We don't have time to tie it on. Just use the clip to hook it to the back of your collar."

Emily quickly hooked the cardboard number to her jacket as Aunt Debby tightened her girth once more. "Okay, Emily, take a deep breath and calm down. Once you go in the ring, you have all the time in the world, okay?"

Emily nodded, watching the horses in the ring

moving, walking and trotting as they all warmed up. "I have to go."

"You'll be fine. Your flat work is outstanding." Aunt Debby stepped back. "Relax!"

Relax. Ha! Emily kicked Moondance into a trot, and they jogged straight into the ring as the judge called out for everyone to walk.

Emily let out a quivering sigh of relief as she convinced a jittery Moondance back to a walk.

They'd made it.

*E*mily adjusted her grip on her reins and eased to a deep seat in the saddle as she tried to collect Moondance. She sank into her heels and began to drive Moondance forward with her seat and her calves, trying to get the mare balanced and collected.

But before she could even begin to get organized, the judge called for a posting trot. Already?

Emily nudged Moondance into a trot, and the mare lurched forward, vibrating with energy from the frantic flight from the van. Emily whispered to Moondance under her breath, attempting to calm the mare as she tried to concentrate on her own form.

She and Moondance were right in front of the judge

when a kid on a small pony cut right in front of them. Moondance threw her head up in surprise and Emily hauled back on the reins to keep from running over the pony. She lost a beat on the trot and had to sit for a stride to get back in rhythm again.

Gritting her teeth, Emily settled again, trying to keep an eye on the crazy pony up ahead, and she managed not to get cut off again for the duration of the trot.

When the judge called for a walk, Emily was back under control—or she was until she found herself suddenly surrounded by a mass of horses whose riders had taken longer to pull their horses back to a walk than Emily and had run up on her.

Moondance jigged sideways, not pleased to be penned in, and then the judge called for a canter.

There was a thunder of hooves around Emily and Moondance as all the novice riders egged their mounts into a canter, and Moondance jumped into a canter before Emily was ready, picking up the wrong lead so Moondance was leading with her outside front leg instead of her inside! A gigantic disaster!

Emily hauled Moondance back to a trot immediately, but the mare was so fired up she took two full strides on the wrong lead before Emily could get her back to a trot. She quickly rebalanced Moondance so the horse picked up the correct lead, and as they eased into a canter, Emily glanced over at the judge—who was staring right at her.

Had she seen their mistake? They were doomed if she had.

The rest of the class continued to be a battle. Emily had never been in the ring with so many other horses, as all dressage tests were individual. Having so many novice riders bumping into her was distracting and unnerving, especially since Moondance was just as agitated.

But Emily fought to keep her form and knew she was by far the best rider in the ring. As long as her wrong lead hadn't been seen, she knew she'd win.

They lined up in the middle of the ring, and she saw Aunt Debby holding on to Sapphire and gesturing to a ring at the far side of the field. Emily nodded, her heart starting to race as she thought of the upcoming class with Sapphire. She sighed in admiration as she watched Aunt Debby lead him toward the other ring, his muscles rippling under his glossy black coat, his braids tight and fantastic. He looked absolutely *gorgeous*.

The judge came forward and announced the sixth-place winner. One hundred twelve.

Emily realized she didn't even know what number she was wearing.

But a girl on a bay pony kicked her mount forward to take the green ribbon, so Emily figured she wasn't one twelve. Not that she'd place sixth, anyway.

Then the fifth place number was called, and a boy on the pony that had cut her off came forward to collect the pink ribbon. If he'd come in fifth after his little move, Emily knew she'd win. Yay, her! No more Maiden class!

The fourth-place white ribbon went to a girl on a pretty chestnut pony, and third place went to a girl on a very attractive bay, and Emily's stomach started to thud. Even at a walk, Emily could tell the girl had good form, and the horse was lovely. And she'd gotten third? Were there good riders in the class she hadn't noticed?

Second was a girl on a beautiful gray horse, and she, too, looked like she had nice form.

A little ball formed in Emily's belly as the judge called out number two-oh-one for first place. She clenched her fists on the reins and looked around to see if anyone else was moving forward.

No one moved.

Was it her? A spark of hope leaped in her chest, and she nudged Moondance forward . . . and the girl on the small pony to her left did the same.

For a second Emily hesitated, and she glanced at the

girl, her stomach dropping when she saw the big grin on the girl's face. Seriously? The girl was about six years old, and the pony didn't even come up to Moondance's shoulder.

But as Emily stopped Moondance, the girl rode out and accepted the blue ribbon from the judge.

Shut out.

She'd been *shut out* of the ribbons in a class she was too good to ride in anyway. Emily whirled Moondance toward the out gate, and then her cheeks got hot when she saw Meredith standing at the in gate on Halo, watching.

Emily bit her lip and nudged Moondance into a faster walk as she reached the in gate, but she couldn't miss seeing the sympathy on Meredith's face.

"What happened?" Meredith asked.

"A disaster." Emily rolled her eyes, too embarrassed to admit the numerous ways she'd blown it. "I have to get to Sapphire for the model class."

Meredith's face closed off slightly at Emily's dismissal. "Oh, okay. Good luck."

"Thanks." Ducking her head, Emily clucked Moondance off to a trot and started weaving across the grounds, fighting back tears of humiliation.

Then she took a deep breath. The day wasn't over

yet. She could still do well with Sapphire and win the over fences Maiden class. Those two classes were actually more important, because Aunt Debby already knew that she could ride on the flat—except when there were a ton of other horses in the ring, apparently. *Yeesh.* What a rookie mistake to get flustered by so many horses . . .

Emily shook her head, trying to put the flat class out of her mind. She pictured Les standing beside her, telling her to calm down and focus, and by the time she reached the other show ring, she was completely in control.

Until she arrived and saw Sapphire already in the ring—being led by Alison? *"What?"* Emily jerked her gaze to the in gate and saw her aunt standing there, looking so proud as she watched Alison and Sapphire. "Aunt Debby!"

Emily cantered Moondance over to her aunt, almost running over two people before hauling Moondance to a stop. "Aunt Debby!"

Her aunt glanced up at her and gave her a nod before turning her attention back to the show ring. "The class was starting and you were still riding. I had to send Alison in." She folded her arms. "He looks fantastic, doesn't he?"

Emily stared at her aunt, unable to stop the tears

from filling her eyes. "But I braided him. I spent two hours yesterday working on his coat and trimming him and practicing—"

Aunt Debby looked up again, and her face softened slightly. "Emily, I'm sorry, but Sapphire is here to be seen. That's the priority, not you being the one to show him. But as I said, he looks fantastic. Great job on the braids." Then Aunt Debby turned back to the show. "I had a couple ask me about him as Alison was leading him in. Cross your fingers."

"Cross my—" Emily clamped her lips shut against the urge to scream and turned back to the ring, clenching her fists when she saw Alison pat Sapphire's neck as she lined him up for the modeling.

He stood perfectly, as Emily had taught him, his ears up and alert, making him look adorable. Who wouldn't want him? Her chest started to ache, and she looked at Aunt Debby. "Who's the couple watching him?"

"Red shirt off to the right."

Emily turned her head and saw a gray-haired man in a red shirt and jeans studying Sapphire intently. Standing next to him was a young woman . . . his daughter, maybe? She was also watching Sapphire, and they both looked interested. *So interested.*

Emily grimaced and turned back to watch Sapphire as Meredith rode up beside her on Halo. "How come you're not showing him?"

"I was too late." Emily couldn't quite keep the annoyance out of her voice.

"Oh, bummer. How's he doing?"

"He hasn't run over the judge yet." He was still being good and didn't make any attempt to knock Alison down. The judge walked around him, inspecting him, and Sapphire didn't even budge.

"Just wait. I'm sure he will," Meredith said cheerfully. "You're lucky you're not showing him. He's a beast out in the ring."

"Really?" Emily glanced at Red Shirt and crossed her fingers behind her back. "Come on, Sapphire," she whispered under her breath.

Then the judge said something to Alison, and Alison started walking him forward, to the end of the ring, and Emily realized it was time for the trot. Alison clucked Sapphire forward, and the two of them jogged down the straightaway. Sapphire's neck was arched, his toes pointed, and his strides sweeping. He was perfect.

Emily glanced over at Red Shirt and saw the woman nudge Red Shirt and whisper to him. He nodded.

Emily felt sick. She looked back at the ring and saw

Sapphire's head lift ever so slightly, and he got a look in his eyes. . . .

"Oh, look," Meredith said. "He's about to go."

Emily caught her breath and leaned forward in eager anticipation. "Uh-oh—"

Before she could finish her words, Sapphire bolted. The reins ripped out of Alison's hands and he streaked across the ring, bucking and squealing. All the other horses broke formation and started dancing nervously as Sapphire galloped by them, nearly running over the judge. His tail was straight up, his ears were back, his head high as he sprinted around the ring, clearly having a fabulous time.

Emily couldn't help but grin as he raced past, planting a solid buck as he ran by Red Shirt, who was now walking away from the ring with his daughter. Aunt Debby muttered something as she ducked underneath the tape and ran into the ring, trying to help the judge and Alison corner Sapphire, who was easily dodging them as he continued to race around.

Emily gave him a thumbs-up as he breezed past again. "Good job, Sapphire," she whispered. "Good boy."

She was sure she saw him wink at her as he ran by.

"Emily!" Aunt Debby shouted. "Get off Moondance,

give him to Meredith, and get in here and help!"

She saw from the look on Aunt Debby's face that she'd seen the thumbs-up, and she winced as she threw her leg over the saddle and slid to the ground. Aunt Debby was not going to appreciate *that* at all.

But as she passed Red Shirt and his daughter, she couldn't quite bring herself to care.

Hadn't she predicted that magic was in the air? Clearly it was.

It took almost twenty minutes to catch Sapphire.
They'd ended up having to corner him with eleven
volunteers, and the only reason they succeeded was
because he'd had his fun and was ready to stop. Meredith
had had to go ride in her second Large Pony class, and
had handed Moondance off to one of the spectators.
The entire class was disrupted, people weren't impressed,
but at least Red Shirt was long gone.

Emily hadn't been able to stop giggling at his antics,
which had really not made Aunt Debby happy.

They'd just caught Sapphire when Meredith appeared
at the in gate on Halo, clutching a blue first-place ribbon
in her hand. "Emily!"

Emily clenched her jaw when she saw the blue ribbon. "What?"

"It's almost your turn in the Maiden over fences class! There are only five horses left in the class, so you have to go soon!"

Emily caught her breath and butterflies jumped in her belly as Aunt Debby came up behind her, clutching Sapphire's reins in her fist. "Go get on Moondance and head to the warm-up area. I'll be right behind you."

Uh-oh . . . Emily could hear from the grittiness in her voice that Aunt Debby was in a severely bad mood. Emily swallowed. "Okay." She glanced at Sapphire, who was dripping with sweat and blowing hard, wanting desperately to give him a hug.

"Emily!"

"Right." She whirled away and ran for the in gate, where a woman in a bright red shirt and hot pink sunglasses was holding Moondance's reins. "Thanks."

"Sure thing, sweetie. Nice effort out there."

Emily swung up on Moondance, barely making it aboard without a leg up, then she turned and headed toward the warm-up area, where horses were racing around, jumping over two verticals set up in the middle. She kicked Moondance into a trot, then hauled her to a stop when someone cut in front of her.

She looked around and suddenly registered the craziness around her. Horses going in every direction, jumping, cantering, trotting. Coaches shouting—

"Emily! Trot the low vertical!" Aunt Debby was standing on the edge of the warm-up area, still holding Sapphire's reins. He was breathing hard, and Emily knew he needed to be cooled down properly.

"Emily! There are only two horses in front of you in the class. Get going!"

She winced at Aunt Debby's aggravated tone and gathered her reins, nudging Moondance into a trot, then quickly stopping when she saw the line of riders waiting to take the jump. With a frown, she pulled up at the end of the line. How was she supposed to warm up properly? Trot for ten seconds. Stand still for five minutes. Trot twenty feet to one of the jumps, then repeat the process? It wouldn't be enough—

Her turn came, and Emily gathered her reins and nudged Moondance into a trot. They were so close to the jump, she barely had time to get into a half-seat before Moondance leaped up. Emily forgot to grab the mane, got left behind, and then jerked forward, nearly pitching over Moondance's shoulder.

She glanced around, but no one seemed to be paying her any attention. The next horse was already jumping the single rail, and Emily hurried to get out of the way.

"Emily! Focus!"

Right. Focus. *Sure.* Emily queued up again and tried to calm her mind and focus on the jumping. This was the class where she needed to concentrate the most, the class where the most was at stake. She frantically recapped all she'd learned in her two jumping lessons—then suddenly remembered that Aunt Debby had warned her this morning she'd have to memorize the order of jumps before she went into the ring!

She jerked her gaze toward the ring and saw a girl on a gray pony jumping. Emily tried to watch the order and still keep an eye on the line as it moved toward the warm-up jump. Diagonal oxer, turn left, take the white picket fence to the brush jump . . .

"Your turn," the girl behind Emily said, and Emily turned back toward the warm-up vertical, realizing it was indeed her turn.

She glanced again at the course as she gathered her reins. Turn left after the brush jump and then head down the diagonal line . . .

She nudged Moondance into a trot and tried to focus on the jump in front of her, then saw a flash of red out of the corner of her eye. She whipped her head to the right and saw Red Shirt talking to Aunt Debby. About Sapphire?

Moondance lurched over the jump, tripped on the rails, and stumbled, jerking Emily off balance. She flew over Moondance's head and landed flat on her back.

Pain ripped down her back, and she tried to suck in her breath, but no air came in. Her lungs wouldn't work! She tried to sit up; pain screamed through her and her body froze. She couldn't move! Tears slid out of her eyes, and she panicked—

"It's okay, Emily." Aunt Debby was suddenly leaning over her, her tanned face creased with worry. "Don't try to move."

Emily shook her head, tried to breathe, couldn't get air, couldn't talk. Sucked in a tiny breath, her body seized up— She grabbed for her aunt's hand, tears flooding her eyes.

"You got the wind knocked out of you, honey." Aunt Debby held her hand tightly, leaning over her. "Just try to relax and it'll come back." She jerked her head up and looked around. "You! Get the ambulance over here!"

Ambulance? Emily tried to shake her head again, but it hurt too much. Tried to suck in more air, but her lungs wouldn't work. She was going to die! Had she broken her back? Punctured her lung? *What was wrong with her?*

"Keep trying to breathe." Aunt Debby's voice was too calm. Didn't she realize Emily was dying? "Breathe, Emily."

Emily's lungs sucked again, trying to get air, and they froze up again. Inhale and freeze. Inhale and freeze. Repeated convulsions as her body fought for oxygen . . .

Suddenly a man was leaning over her, a little emblem on his shirt indicating he was a medical guy. "Hi there, Emily. You're going to be fine. Does your back hurt?"

Emily managed a nod while her lungs continued to seize up on her, and he nodded. "Keep breathing." Someone else leaned over Emily, blocking the sun, and then they wrapped something around her neck.

She clawed it, suffocating, panic racing through her, and the man caught her hands. "Okay, Emily, try to calm down. You can breathe just fine. It's only a collar to immobilize your neck until we know for sure it's okay."

A broken neck? She might have a broken neck? She tried to shake her head, nearly screamed with the pain, and sucked in more air, and this time she got a little breath before her lungs seized up.

"See? You'll be okay. You're getting more air already."

He looked up. "Get the stretcher over here."

Stretcher? "No . . ." She managed to gasp the one word, and he ignored her, and suddenly she found herself sliding onto a stiff surface. Pain shot through her back again, and she gasped, Aunt Debby huddling behind the ambulance guy.

Aunt Debby leaned over her and took her hand. "It's okay, Em. I'm going to call your dad, and he'll meet us at the hospital. I'm going to ride over with you in the ambulance. You'll be fine."

"No . . ." Emily tried to sit up, but she couldn't. Something was holding her down. Straps! They'd tied her down! Panic raced through her again, and she started to fight, her breath coming easier now, but her back still hurting so badly. "Have to ride—"

"No, you don't." Aunt Debby's voice was firm, and she shook her head. "You are going to the hospital."

Aunt Debby stepped back, and the medical guy was there again, and they were all talking and ignoring her, and then she heard Aunt Debby ask if Emily's back was broken and the guy said he didn't know yet.

And that's when Emily started to cry.

"Okay, Emily, how are you feeling?"

Emily managed a trembly smile at the doctor. The doctors had determined that Emily was going to be fine (according to them), and Aunt Debby had confirmed Emily's dad was on his way. The two adults had decided that Aunt Debby should go back to the show, because neither of them liked leaving Alison and Meredith alone there, in case something happened to *them*.

So, Aunt Debby had left, but Emily's dad hadn't appeared yet, and it had been *forever*. The white walls were closing in on her, the smell of antiseptic harsh on her nose. She could hear the sounds of whispers, of tears, of low voices in the hall. "Fine." She sniffled, trying to keep from crying. "I'm fine."

"Good." The doctor pulled up a seat next to the bed Emily was in. She'd introduced herself as Dr. Truax, and she had bright red hair pulled into a bun, but lots of strands were falling out. Her eyes were blue and she was young. And so nice. She'd come in to see Emily every few minutes and had even brought her a copy of *Teen People*. If it weren't for Dr. Truax, Emily knew she would have totally fallen apart.

"Is your dad here yet?"

"No." Emily bit her lip to fight the tears. Where was her dad? She'd been there almost two hours!

Dr. Truax's forehead wrinkled, but she patted Emily's leg. "Now, don't you worry, Emily. I'm sure he'll be here soon." She pulled out a plate of brownies from behind her back. "I stole them from the employee break room. One of the nurses makes them from scratch. Triple chocolate fudge with homemade frosting. Want some?"

"Ooh . . ." Emily leaned forward to peer at the plate. "Really? They look so good."

"They are good. Help yourself." Dr. Truax picked up a brownie and took a big bite, chocolate crumbles falling down the front of her white jacket. "Mmm . . ."

Emily giggled and picked up a brownie. "You have fudge on your clothes." She held up the sticky brownie in two hands and sank her teeth into it. Rich, gooey, warm chocolate oozed over her tongue. "Ohmygoth," she said with a full mouth. "Thith ith the betht . . ." She swallowed. "The best brownie *ever*."

Dr. Truax nodded. "So worth some fudge on the shirt front, don't you think?"

"For sure." Emily shoved the rest of the brownie in her mouth. "Can I have more?"

The doctor winked at Emily. "They're all for you."

"Oh, *cool*." Emily helped herself to another and sighed with delight as it melted in her mouth. "This almost makes the whole hospital trip worthwhile—"

The door slammed open and there stood her dad, wearing jeans and boots. "Emily!" His hair was totally scruffy, he had bags under his eyes, and his skin was an ashen gray. He looked sick. He looked terrified. *He looked like the best thing she'd ever seen.*

The tears flared up and spilled out, and the brownie hit the floor. "Daddy!"

"Oh, Em!" He was across the hospital room and had her in his arms in a split second.

Emily fell into him, unable to stop the sobs that exploded when his arms closed around her, protecting her, making her safe forever and ever. "What took you so long? I've been waiting and waiting and waiting—"

"Sweetie, I'm so sorry it took me so long to get here." He kissed the top of her head like he used to do when she was little when he used to put her to bed, and Emily sagged against him.

"Don't leave me," she whispered, scrunching her eyes closed as she buried her face in the rough material of his shirt.

"Never." He hugged her tightly, twisting her back.

She squawked with pain, and he quickly released her, his face white. "What's wrong? Tell me."

"No, don't let go of me." She couldn't keep the whine out of her voice, but she needed him to hold her so badly.

"Excuse me," the doctor interrupted. "I'm Dr. Truax. You must be Emily's dad?"

"Yes." He sat next to Emily on the bed and wrapped his arm carefully around her. "What's going on?"

Emily leaned into him, so happy he was finally there. She sighed, knowing that she didn't have to be strong anymore. He'd take care of her.

Dr. Truax wrapped the brownies back up and handed them to Emily. "She'll be fine."

Emily's dad tightened his arm around Emily. "Really?"

His voice cracked slightly.

"Really." Dr. Truax nodded. "She has a bad bruise on her back. Looks like she landed on a rock, maybe. She also got the wind knocked out of her, but she's breathing fine now, right, Emily?"

Emily managed a nod as she sagged against him.

"Give her back a few days to heal up, and she's good to go." Dr. Truax ruffled Emily's hair. "She's free to leave, of course. Try to stay in the saddle next time, young lady."

Emily shuddered at the thought of jumping again. It had been such a tiny jump, and she'd been hurt so badly. . . .

Nope. There wasn't going to be a next time.

She was done jumping.

Emily eased gingerly into the booth at Jake's Burgers an hour later, where she and her dad had stopped for dinner on the way home from the hospital. She'd fallen asleep the minute they'd gotten in the car and had woken up as her dad had pulled into the parking lot.

She was still groggy but felt a little calmer.

Calm enough to be mad.

Her dad slid opposite her and gave her a worried look. "How do you feel?"

"Why did it take you so long to get to the hospital?"

He winced. "I'm so sorry, hon. I left the minute Aunt Debby called me, but the hospital was a lot closer to the show than it was to the farm. Trust me, I broke a few laws getting there."

"If you'd been at the show, you would have been there with me the whole time. Do you know how scared I was? Aunt Debby *left me there.*" Her voice broke, and she snapped her mouth shut. She was *so tired* of crying.

"I know, Em, I know." He ground his teeth and rubbed his hand over his eyes. "Believe me, it was killing me, knowing you were there alone."

"Aunt Debby—"

"Aunt Debby couldn't leave the girls alone at the show, in case something else happened. Once she knew you were going to be okay, we both felt that it was important for her to get back there." He interrupted quickly, almost as if he were trying to convince himself. His voice was low and tense, rough. "She had no choice."

Emily snorted. "No, she had a choice. You both did, and you both chose the show and two perfectly healthy girls instead of me in a hospital, possibly *dying*!"

Her dad's eyebrows went up. "Oh, *Emily*." He sounded so incredibly sorry. "You thought you were dying?"

"How did I know? I couldn't breathe!" She recalled again the panic, the pain, and started to hunch into a little ball. Her old dad, the dad in New Jersey, would *never* have left her alone in the hospital for two hours. She never would have gotten hurt this badly in a dressage show, and Les would have made sure she was organized, not two hours late. "Dad?"

"Yes, sweetie?" His voice was soft as he reached across the table and stroked her hair.

"I want to go home."

"Back to the farm?"

"No." She raised her eyes to his. "To New Jersey. I want everything back the way it used to be. I want you to have time for me again, I want to ride Rhapsody in the dressage show next weekend, and I want a coach who won't send me off to the hospital by myself." Her lower lip was trembling, but she couldn't stop it. "I want to go back." *Because in New Jersey, I matter.*

Her dad's hand dropped from her hair and he leaned back in his seat, a suddenly wary look on his face.

An expression that made her stomach turn. "Dad?"

"I, um . . ." He cleared his throat. "I thought

we agreed that we wanted to stay at the farm for a while. . . ."

Emily sat up, gasped at the shot of pain, and then looked at her dad. *"What did you do?"*

"I gave up the lease on Rhapsody. He isn't yours anymore."

Tears filled her eyes before she could stop them as the pain of the ultimate betrayal knifed through her. "You didn't!"

Her dad nodded. "It makes sense, Em. I can't keep paying for him if we're not going to be there and he needs someone to take care of him. Your friend Jenny Smith picked up the lease—"

"Jenny?" Oh, no! Not Jenny! Emily could just see Jenny's smug face laughing at her as Jenny finally got the horse they'd both coveted. "How could you do that to me without talking to me first?"

"Emily—"

"This is all because of the farm! You used to be my best friend, and we used to be there for each other. You would *never* have done something like this to me. Never!" Her stomach ached. "Aunt Debby's changing you. You aren't my dad anymore—"

"Emily!" Her dad leaned forward. "I understand it's been a tough day for you, and I agree I should have been at the hospital the whole time, but I still love you, and I haven't changed. I have to make the decisions that are best for us—"

"For you! Not me!" She shook her head, unable to stop her hands from shaking. "How can I trust you anymore? I can't. You're on *her* side now. Not mine. I don't matter."

"Of course you matter—"

She met his gaze. "Why didn't you tell me about Rhapsody before you did it?"

Her dad seemed to sag in his seat. "I knew it would upset you."

"So you lied to me so you could do what you wanted without even telling me? Even though you knew Rhapsody was my dream?"

Her dad frowned. "I thought you had new dreams."

"No, Dad. You do." She folded her arms. She bit her lip, refusing to look at him, too upset to talk anymore. Her dad, her best friend for her whole life . . . she couldn't trust him anymore.

And Aunt Debby had tried to sell Sapphire without telling her, and then she'd teamed up with her dad to abandon her in the hospital.

It was official. She was on her own.

The entire ride home from dinner was silence.

Finally Emily had her dad all to herself, and they were both too upset to talk. Emily simply stared out the window, watching the city change to fields and trees—land that had mesmerized her only a few short weeks ago when she'd first arrived and now . . . it made her want to cry. Why couldn't something that was so close to her dreams actually make her happy? A farm, beautiful pastures, horses, and family? Why weren't they enough?

She didn't know. She just knew they weren't, and it didn't matter how badly she wanted them to be.

Because she did. She really, really did.

Her dad pulled up at the barn as the sun was beginning to set. Emily saw that the van was back and already parked alongside the barn.

"Emily." Her dad turned toward her. "I'm really sorry—"

"It doesn't matter."

She threw her door open and hadn't even set her foot on the ground when Aunt Debby shouted her name and came running out of the barn. "Emily!"

Emily grabbed the plate of brownies she'd taken from the hospital and eased out of the car, then gasped with pain when Aunt Debby grabbed her and hugged her.

"Oh! Sorry." Aunt Debby quickly released her, gazing at her with a look Emily couldn't decipher. "You're really okay? I've been so worried."

Emily frowned, not believing Aunt Debby's show of concern. "Yeah, I'm sure you were." She shifted out of her aunt's grasp. "Did you sell Sapphire today?"

"No." Her aunt sighed. "The buyer I'd arranged to watch him wasn't interested after his antics in the class."

Emily raised her brows. "You arranged that ahead of time? *That's* why you decided to take Sapphire to the show at the last minute? Because a buyer wanted to see him?"

"Yes—"

"And you didn't tell me? You know how I feel about him and you didn't tell me that's why I was getting him ready?"

Aunt Debby frowned. "Emily, you know he's for sale."

"Oh, and that makes it okay?"

"Em—" Her dad gave a low warning. "Aunt Debby doesn't need to account for everything she does at the farm."

"No, she doesn't, does she? Neither of you do. I am *so tired* of you guys justifying *everything* for the good of the barn! Don't you realize that there are other things that matter besides the farm?"

Emily's throat was tight, and she turned away, not wanting them to see the tears in her eyes. "I'm going to see Sapphire." She broke into a run, her back screaming in protest, but she didn't stop when they shouted after her, telling her to come back.

She had to see Sapphire. To know he was still there. To assure herself that they hadn't stolen him from her without telling her.

She ran past Halo's stall and saw three blue ribbons, a red ribbon, and a championship ribbon hanging from his stall door. Emily stopped for a moment and stared at all the ribbons. Ribbons she'd thought she'd be taking home.

After a few seconds, she picked one up and flipped it over. Someone had written LARGE PONY UNDER SADDLE on the back of the red ribbon. She picked up a blue ribbon and saw it was for the Open 11–14 over fences.

She suddenly felt completely embarrassed. Meredith had won her Open equitation class and been champion in Large Pony. Emily hadn't been able to place in the Maiden on the flat and hadn't even made it into the ring for her over fences class.

"Heard you blew it today."

She turned around at the sound of her cousin Kyle's voice. He was watching her with amusement. "Why do you have to be a jerk?"

He blinked. "What?"

"A jerk! Why do you have to be a jerk?"

His eyes were wide, his face shocked, in a reasonable imitation of someone pretending he had no idea what she was talking about, but she didn't buy it. "Leave me alone."

She shoved the blue ribbon back onto Halo's door, then stormed past Kyle. *I will not show him he matters.* Tears were brimming in her eyes by the time she rounded the corner to Sapphire's aisle, and she tried to run but had to slow when her back protested.

His stall door was open. Was he not in there?

She hobbled the rest of the way and yanked the door open.

Alison was in his stall, taking out his braids. "Oh, hi, Emily. How are you feeling?"

Phew. He is still here.

Emily set the plate of brownies on the floor next to the door and stepped inside. "I'll do that." Sapphire turned his head on the cross ties to look at her, and he snorted softly. His coat was still shiny and bright, and he was wearing a fly sheet from the show. He even still had his wraps on, a wrap job that wasn't nearly as good as Emily would have done for him. His wraps were loose, not tight and perfect the way he deserved. No one else could take care of him the way she could. *No one.* "I'll finish him up."

"No, it's okay. I know you're hurt so—"

"I'll do it." Emily couldn't keep her voice from wavering, and she saw Alison's face flicker in acknowledgment. She laid her palm on Sapphire's nose and rubbed the velvety skin, barely able to keep herself from hugging him, from completely falling apart in front of Alison. "Really. I'd like to take care of him."

"Okay." Alison stepped down off the stool. "Keep his wraps on. After his mad sprint in the ring, my mom wants him wrapped overnight to support his legs, in case he tweaked the ankle he hurt before."

Emily nodded, biting her lip as Alison walked out into the aisle. "Okay."

"Emily!" They both turned as Meredith flew into the stall. She still had her breeches on, but she was wearing sneakers and a T-shirt over her choker. She threw her arms around Emily, and Emily yelped with pain.

"Oh, gosh! I'm so sorry." Meredith quickly let go, but her dark brown eyes were fastened on Emily. "Where are you hurt? Is it bad? Do you need surgery?"

Emily warmed at Meredith's apparent concern, noting Alison pausing in the aisle to hear her answer. Alison looked curious; Meredith looked worried, scared even. So she faced Meredith and ignored Alison. "I'm okay. Just hurt my back."

"Really? You're *really* okay?"

Emily nodded, wrapping her arm around Sapphire's neck and leaning against him, feeling his soft, warm coat against her cheek, inhaling the scent of pine shavings from his coat, as he'd clearly been lying down since his return.

Meredith seemed to sag with relief. "Good, because

I can't tell you how scary it was to see you lying there and then get carted off in the ambulance. I've been freaking out all day!" She looked at Alison. "Was it the scariest thing ever or what?"

Alison shrugged. "She got the wind knocked out of her. It happens."

Emily narrowed her eyes at her cousin. She thought she'd been *dying*, and all her cousin could say was "it happens"?

"I already unbraided Moondance for you," Alison said. "But you might want to check on her."

Emily tensed at the mention of Moondance, hoping they wouldn't mention the one class she'd ridden in. "Um, thanks."

Meredith grinned. "Oh my gosh, Emily, you should have seen Alison and Icy! She ended up riding him in a couple classes, and he was awesome. They won both of them, and she had three different people ask Debby where they'd found him! He's absolutely *gorgeous* and so good."

Alison's face lit up. "He was brilliant, wasn't he? And you did so well with Halo! You're so going to be ranked this summer with him."

"You think?" Meredith beamed. "That would be so cool. I'd love to qualify for Harrisburg at the end of the year, not that Debby would ever take us to Pennsylvania for the show, you know? Or even Washington. They're both so far."

"But if we both qualified, it might be worth it to make the trip."

"You think? Are you going to try to qualify with Icy?"

"Next year, maybe. We could go to Arizona for the winter circuit to get some points."

Meredith squealed, and they started to talk away. "Seriously? Is your mom thinking about taking us down there?"

"Now that we have Icy, yeah. Icy and Halo could compete, you know?" They turned the corner and disappeared, but Emily could still hear them. "And it would be great exposure. If we could have Sapphire ready to show by then, think of all the exposure. . . ."

Their voices faded, leaving Emily alone with Sapphire. For a long moment, she stared after them, feeling completely invisible. The good feeling from Meredith's initial concern had completely faded in the face of their talk about their success and the fact they both had completely forgotten Emily was there.

Sapphire snorted quietly and nudged Emily.

"Oh, Sapphire." She unhooked him from the cross ties and hugged him as he pressed his face to her chest, for once not trying to knock her down. She pressed her face to his, rubbing her cheeks over his soft ears, holding him against her. "I matter to you, don't I?"

He snorted and pressed harder against her.

"You were so smart to be bad today in that class, Sapphire. Thank you for doing that," she whispered. "I can't tell you how much it meant to me."

He lifted his head to look at her, then lifted his upper lip in a grin that she couldn't help but laugh at. "You are such a goof." She scratched behind his ears and giggled when he pointed his head at the ceiling and wiggled his lip with delight. "But a smart, gorgeous goof." She stopped scratching, and he dropped his head to look at her, the expression in his brown eyes clearly requesting additional scratching.

"And I'm so glad you screwed up Aunt Debby's plans to sell you. It looks like we have lots of time now." She fisted his mane, gripping tightly as she leveled a determined gaze at him. "There's no way I'm going to let her sell you, Sapphire. We'll find a way, won't we?"

He stomped his foot and swished his tail, and the tightness finally began to ease from her chest. "Just so you know, you're my best friend."

He pressed his face to her belly, gently, as if he knew she was injured and fragile, and she knew then that she could always count on him.

Always.

Then she thought of his antics in the model class, and she grimaced. Would Sapphire have taken off like that if Emily had been showing him, or would he have been good? She'd liked to think he would have given her what she needed—

He gave her a hard shove and knocked her onto her butt.

She frowned as she stared up at him. "Do I need to be careful about what I trust you for, Sapphire?"

He turned his head toward the door and flared his nostrils. Then he nickered and popped his head out the door, snuffling the plate of brownies. Emily gingerly hopped to her feet. "Oh, I forgot! I brought you treats!" She grabbed the plate and handed Sapphire a carrot and popped another brownie in her mouth.

She grinned as they chomped. "I know you wouldn't have let me down in that class, Sapphire. You and me, beautiful. We're on the same team. High five." She held up her hand for a high five, and he licked the chocolate off her palm in what she decided to take as an affirmative.

They'd met over chocolate, and they were bonding over chocolate. Chocolate buddies never let each other down.

*E*mily was up and dressed before six o'clock the next morning, her back too sore for her to sleep. It felt almost normal when she was vertical, so she decided to get up and get going for the day, hoping she could slip in and take Sapphire on a walk before the barn got active. A little private time before dealing with everyone.

But when she walked into the kitchen, Aunt Debby was there eating oatmeal and reading the latest issue of *The Chronicle of the Horse*. She looked up when Emily entered the kitchen. "You'll ride Moondance in your lesson today."

Emily tensed. "My lesson?"

Aunt Debby nodded. "Your lesson. We'll talk about

what happened at the show and then work on some more jumping—"

"My back still hurts," Emily interrupted. "I can't." She thought about jumping again and . . . No. She wasn't ready.

Aunt Debby stopped chewing and looked at her for a moment, studying Emily so intently that Emily began to feel uncomfortable. "Okay, I'll give you a day, but the doctor said you are okay, so we'll do a lesson tomorrow. Eight o'clock on Moondance."

"Can I ride Sapphire?"

"No." Aunt Debby closed the magazine and looked at her. "So, you want to talk about your flat class?"

Emily glanced longingly for the back door. "I don't know what happened."

Aunt Debby raised her brows. "No?"

"I picked up the wrong lead," Emily mumbled.

Aunt Debby nodded. "I saw that. We're on the same team, Emily. Don't hide things from me." She leaned forward. "Emily, I know you were expecting great things at the show, but it's okay that you didn't win. This type of riding is different, and you need to give yourself time. You'll get there."

Emily gritted her teeth, hating that she had no rebuttal. She'd proven her aunt right, that she didn't deserve to be in higher classes.

"Now, I'm thinking that part of the confusion was that there were so many other horses in the flat class, so I want you to ride Moondance on Thursday at ten. I teach a group lesson then, and the ring will be crowded. I want you to participate."

Emily tensed at the thought of trying to maneuver around all those horses again, felt the same franticness that she'd experienced at the show, and she shook her head. "My back—"

"When you're ready then." Aunt Debby stood up. "If you aren't riding, what's your plan today?"

"I was going to spend some time with T.J., hang out with Sapphire, and then check on Hercules."

Aunt Debby nodded, completely ignoring the T.J. comment. "Good. Let me know how Hercules is." She tossed her bowl in the dishwasher then left, letting the door slam shut behind her.

For a second Emily was tempted to race after her and beg for the lesson at ten o'clock, but then she thought of jumping, thought of that moment when she hadn't been able to breathe or move, her panic and fear . . . and she shook her head.

No. Too soon.

There was a whicker from the direction of the sink,

and Emily looked toward the window, then smiled when she saw Max's grizzled gray head sticking through the frame. "Hi, Max."

His ears perked up, and she went to the fridge and grabbed him a head of iceberg lettuce and set it on the counter. He snorted his appreciation and began munching it, spreading lettuce bits all over the counter. She watched him for a moment and saw that he was keeping his eyes on her. "You're lonely, aren't you? You miss Grandpa, don't you?"

She rested her elbows on the counter and watched him eat, realizing that she knew exactly how he felt. Alone.

Then there was a scuffle from outside, and suddenly Sapphire shoved his head in through the window as well. "Sapphire!" Her heart lightened. "You got out again! You're such a bad boy!"

He snorted unapologetically and jerked his head, as if to beckon her out of the kitchen.

"Okay, okay. I'm coming!" She grabbed an apple off the counter, filched a lead shank by the door, and then headed out of the kitchen.

Sapphire was standing at the back door waiting for her the moment she stepped onto the porch. She hooked a lead shank to his halter. "You want to come with me to visit Hercules? Maybe you can show him that I'm not so scary."

He pranced in place happily, his ears perked and his tail up as Max lumbered around the corner. She patted Max. "You want to come, too? We can all visit Hercules."

Max sighed his assent, and she chortled at him, then slung her arms over the backs of each horse as the three of them began to head toward the back pasture: Sapphire's well-muscled shiny black coat and Max's old swayback. She heard someone shouting for Sapphire, and she yelled back that she had found him, laughing as Sapphire winked at her. "You're such a troublemaker. You know that, don't you?"

He pranced slightly, not enough to jar her back but enough to make her laugh, and Max gave Sapphire a baleful look, as if he couldn't deal with such energy and impertinence.

"Oh, Max, give him a break! He's actually quite charming."

Max ignored them both, plodding along at a slow, steady pace, as if he were leading the way to their destination—with them but not truly committed to them. It was like he was putting up with them because he had no one else to be with, and they were better than nothing.

Yeesh. Even Max didn't think she was anything special.

Then Sapphire turned his head back to look at her, and she saw his chocolate eyes fasten on her. "Yeah, except for you. I won't forget."

Sapphire swished his tail, then he did a little dance that dislodged her arm from his back and made Max roll his eyes. Sapphire danced again and looked at Emily, so she did a little jig like he'd done.

His tail went up, and he pranced again, then looked at her.

She laughed and danced again, this time waving her arms and wiggling her head like he'd done.

He snorted and spun in a little circle, ripping the lead shank out of her hand before he came to a stop, looking at her expectantly.

With a giggle, she shimmied in place then spun around like he'd done, totally cracking up by the time she was facing him again. "You are soooo funny, Sapphire!" She grabbed the lead shank with a light heart and started back toward the pasture again, this time with a grin, feeling truly happy for the first time in days.

The sky was a gorgeous blue, not a cloud to be seen. The air was fresh and crisp, and she could see endless fields before her. Tall, thick pine trees were hiding birds that were singing, and up ahead were pastures full of horses. And beside her was her best friend. "Everything's going to be just fine, isn't it?"

He snorted in agreement, and her heart leaped with joy.

Then she realized they were passing a trailer full of extra jump standards. She looked at them as they walked past, at the white wood, at the little black cups for the rails to sit in, at the red-and-white-striped rails on the ground. Exactly the kind of rail Moondance had tripped on.

How badly would she have been hurt if the jump had been bigger? Would she even have survived?

Sapphire nickered softly, and she looked at him. "Maybe it's okay that Aunt Debby won't let me jump you. Maybe I'm not meant to be a jumper, you know?" But even as she said it, she knew she didn't want it to be true. She wanted to jump. She did.

But as she looked back over her shoulder at the pile of jumps again and felt the ache in her back . . .

Max whinnied and stopped beside her. She jerked her gaze to see where he was looking and saw Hercules standing at the fence, his little head peeking over the bottom rail, watching them approach.

She tightened her grip on Sapphire's lead shank.

"That little guy needs us, Sapphire. You up for the challenge?"

Sapphire snorted, but it was Max who walked forward. It was Max who led the way.

She held Sapphire back for a second, letting Max approach the little pony. Hercules watched him intently, his dark eyes fastened on Max.

The old gray horse reached the pony, and for a long moment they simply stared at each other, nostrils flaring as they scented each other.

Then Max whickered softly and lowered his head to Hercules's level and touched the little pony's nose gently with his own.

And Emily knew her scared little pony had found a friend.

*E*mily whispered to Sapphire to be quiet, and they carefully walked up behind Max, to where the old gray horse was trading secrets with Hercules. "Hi, sweetie." She kept her voice low and friendly. "It's good to see you again."

Hercules jerked his head up, his eyes wide, then he turned and sprinted away from her with more panic than spirit. She sighed as she came up next to Max, who was watching Hercules through the fence. "Why is he so scared?"

Neither Max nor Sapphire told her an answer, but Hercules circled back around and came to a stop a moderate distance from them. His little feet were splayed, his head up and his nostrils flaring, but he was watching Max closely.

Emily narrowed her eyes, and after a minute of thinking, she nudged Max's shoulder. "Come on."

She and Sapphire led the way to the gate, and she opened it as Hercules bolted across the paddock away from her. Then she led Sapphire into the paddock and Max followed. Sapphire waited patiently while she locked the gate, but Max headed straight for Hercules.

Hercules waited for Max to reach him, his brown eyes fastened on Max so desperately that Emily wanted to cry for him.

She unhooked Sapphire, but he stayed by her side, curious as she walked up to Max. She intentionally ignored Hercules, but the little pony still bolted away as she scratched Max's withers. Hercules stood about forty feet away, scenting her and prancing nervously as she patted Max.

After about fifteen minutes, Hercules sidled up closer, easing his way beside Max, keeping the old gray horse between himself and Emily. She kept talking to Max, and slowly she slid around behind Max until she was face-to-face with Hercules.

He froze, his body went rigid, and she saw the terror in his eyes as he pressed himself up against Max.

"Hey, little guy, it's okay." She reached out to him, and he started to shake so hard she was afraid he was going to shatter. "Okay, I won't touch you." She let her hand drop as Sapphire came up behind her and rested his chin on her shoulder, studying Hercules. "See? Sapphire knows I'm nice."

She didn't move any closer to Hercules, but she didn't back up, either.

Instead she kept talking to him, scratching Max and Sapphire and telling Hercules about her bad day at the show. "So, anyway, I totally know how you feel because I learned I can't trust anyone here, either. You and me, Hercules, we're the same."

She noticed that the shakes had eased off, and his body wasn't quite as rigid as it had been. But he was still watching her carefully, and she could tell he was ready to bolt if she made any sudden moves. But she was totally encouraged because he was only a few feet from her and he wasn't running away.

Emily grinned cheerfully at him. "Okay, so I know you're probably dying for me to come on over there and give you a bath, but gosh, look at the time. I don't think we can swing it. You don't mind if we put it off to later, do you?"

Hercules gave her a wary look, one ear angling

slightly toward her, to show he was listening. "So I'm psyched we made progress, aren't you? I'll bring Max back with me later today, and we can all hang out again, huh? Maybe watch a movie, eat some popcorn, gossip a little?" She suddenly remembered the apple, and she dug it out of her pocket and held it out to him. "Want some apple?"

Hercules threw up his head in a panic and scuttled backward at her movement.

"Shoot. Sorry." Emily squatted and rolled it across the grass toward him. It banged into his front foot, and he immediately whirled around and sprinted away from her. She wrinkled her nose as she watched him go. So much for the progress they'd made. "Okay, so clearly I need to work on my soothing and calming approach, huh? Don't worry, Hercules," she called out. "We'll get there."

There was a crunch, and she looked down to see Sapphire and Max munching on the apple. Well, Sapphire had claimed it, but he'd dropped half of it when he'd bitten into it, and Max had scooped up most of the rest of it. "Hey!" She grabbed the remaining piece off the ground. "That's for Hercules! Shame on you!" She hooked Sapphire back up to the lead shank, grabbed Max's mane, and started to tug them toward the gate, tossing the last piece of apple at Hercules before heading out the gate.

When she looked back, Hercules was already at the apple, munching on it. He'd gone for it far sooner than he'd mustered the courage to go for the carrot yesterday, and she was still in sight.

He lifted his head to look at her, little bits of mushed apple decorating the whiskers on his chin. He looked so little and vulnerable, a tiny pony in that big paddock, so scared of the world.

Emily leaned on the fence and peered over at him. "You and I are going to make a great team, little guy. By the time I'm done with you, you're going to be sticking your head in the kitchen window at dinnertime like Max does. Trust me, the entire head of iceberg lettuce will make it completely worthwhile to put up with the family dinner."

His ears pricked forward for a split second, and then he turned and ran off, his stubby little legs pumping to get him as far away from her as he could.

She rested her chin on the fence rail as she watched him. "You're going to challenge me, aren't you?" He came to a stop on the other side of the paddock and ignored her.

She sighed, realizing that if she didn't find a way to

reach him, poor Hercules was going to spend his whole life alone and terrified, when there were people who wanted to love him and help him right there, if only he could let them near.

She clenched her fists and hopped off the fence to go back to the barn. She would *not* let that happen to him. Somehow, someway, she'd find a way to help him. And she wasn't going to do it for Aunt Debby, or to prove herself capable. Emily was going to do it because she knew what it was like to be scared, and no one deserved to feel the way Emily did, even a little pony.

One of them had to be happy, and she was going to make sure it was Hercules.

16

*E*mily took Max and Sapphire to visit Hercules three more times that day, but she couldn't even get close enough to Hercules to see the color of his eyes. He was agitated and nervous, and only Max could calm him down when Emily was there, but even with Max, he wouldn't let Emily near him. By the third trip, Emily was starting to have some difficulty keeping up her positive attitude, and she was getting frustrated.

Not *at* Hercules but with herself, for being unable to reach him. In one weak moment she had even wondered if Aunt Debby and her dad had been right to limit her independence at the barn, but she'd quickly ditched that idea.

Minor setbacks. She'd get through them. She always did.

By the end of the day, Max wouldn't even leave the ring, so she locked him in with Hercules and some food and water so the two of them would be taken care of for the night, at least feeling better that Hercules had a friend.

Sapphire had been thoroughly entertained by all the trips back and forth, and he'd been excellent, not once trying to rip the lead shank out of her hand and bolt away. She'd taken off his wraps, and his legs were cool and not swollen, so she was confident there'd been no lasting damage from his romp around the ring.

She was leaning on his stall door, watching him eat dinner when she heard her aunt calling her. Emily made a face, then turned toward her aunt. "What?"

"How's Hercules?"

Emily filled her aunt in on the situation and saw her aunt's face soften in sympathy for the little pony. True sympathy, and she remembered her aunt really did care about the horses.

Emily suddenly was hit with a feeling of intense yearning, of longing. To see her aunt look at her like that, just once, like she really cared. Like they were the family that everyone kept claiming they were.

"You think he'll follow Max down to the barn?"

Emily blinked, trying to remember what they'd been talking about. "Who?"

Her aunt raised her brows. "Hercules."

"Oh, right. I don't know. Maybe."

Aunt Debby nodded thoughtfully. "Tomorrow morning, bring Max to the barn and let Hercules follow. See if you can get the two of them into a stall."

"A stall?" Emily frowned. "Won't that scare him?"

"We need to get a look at him, Em. Make sure he's healthy. We'll be careful. How about after your lesson? You can go get him?"

"My lesson?" She kicked her toe in the dirt, thinking of the jump standards in back that she'd passed. "I'm not sure—"

"I am. Lesson in the morning. No debate." And then Aunt Debby walked away without even waiting for Emily's response.

Emily stared after her, chewing her lower lip as Sapphire stuck his head out the door. "Sapphire?" Her voice sounded so small she didn't even recognize it. "I don't think I want to jump," she whispered to him, then she swallowed hard as she wrapped her arm around his head and rested her cheek against his. She'd kept herself so busy with Hercules and the other horses today that she hadn't even thought about jumping, but now . . . "I'm not ready—"

"Scared?" Kyle's head suddenly popped up from the next stall, startling both of them. Sapphire snorted and jumped back, clanking his jaw into Emily's head with a smack that made her reel.

She rubbed her head where Sapphire had whacked her. "No, I'm not scared. Why are you hiding in there?"

"Wasn't hiding." He held up a hoof pick and made a face. "Mom's making me clean all the rescue horses' hooves today for playing my Game Boy during dinner last night. Want to help?"

"No, but it does make me feel better to know that she gives you grief, too." It did, actually. Emily wasn't accustomed to having siblings who were facing the same thing she was when it came to the adults in the family. It made her feel a little less picked on. "Doesn't it bug you?"

"Yeah, but you never show it. That's the trick." Kyle leaned over on the door, hanging his elbows over the lip. "So you crashed bad, huh? Is that why you're freaking about jumping again?"

Was she freaking? Emily realized that Kyle was sort of right, and that was not good. First, that Kyle was right, and second, that she was freaking about horses.

Her true love? That had to end *now*. Emily pulled her shoulders back. "I'm not scared. I'm going to do the lesson tomorrow." She would, too. She'd never been scared of horses in her life, and she wasn't about to start now.

"I hate riding," Kyle said.

Emily blinked in surprise. "You do? Seriously?"

"Yeah. Game Boy's way better than riding." Kyle gave her a pained look that was so melodramatic she had to stifle a giggle. "When I turn eighteen and move out, I'm going to play Game Boy all day every day and never touch a horse ever again."

Kyle's words made Emily think of her dad and how he'd walked away from the family barn. Had he been like Kyle? Pushed into horses until he hated it? She couldn't imagine hating horses. Then she frowned, thinking of how Aunt Debby was forcing her into the lesson. If she didn't like horses in the first place, living on the farm . . . well, it might be kind of yucky. "Your mom does get kind of pushy when it comes to horses, doesn't she?"

Kyle rolled his eyes. "Um, *yeah*. I—"

"Kyle!" Aunt Debby's voice rang out down the aisle.

Kyle winced. "Gotta go. Later, cuz." He jogged

down the aisle, hoof pick swinging in his fingers as he disappeared around the corner.

"Cuz," huh? For the first time ever, Emily wasn't completely disgusted by the fact Kyle was related to her. It made her feel good to know that someone else struggled under Aunt Debby's rule, especially her own kid. Made Emily feel like maybe she wasn't alone. Not that Kyle would support her, but at least he was suffering with her.

She turned back to Sapphire and started when she saw Caitlyn standing there. Her littlest cousin.

"Hi, Emily."

"Hi."

"So, I heard you got hurt." Caitlyn's brow furrowed.

"I'm fine."

Her cousin nodded. "That's good. I like you. I don't want you to get hurt."

Emily couldn't help but grin at the serious expression on Caitlyn's face. "Thanks." She hesitated. "Did you really win a Maiden class?"

Caitlyn bobbed her head again. "I really did. Do you want to know how to do it? I'll tell you my secret."

Emily couldn't help but laugh. Somehow, Caitlyn didn't make her feel bad or silly or embarrassed, even though she'd apparently done far better in shows than

Emily. "Please, tell me your secret."

Caitlyn leaned forward and lowered her voice. "My mom told me that I had to connect with my pony to win, so before the class, I promised Copper, the pony I was riding, I'd give him an ice cream cone if we won. So he was perfect." She put her finger over her lips. "Don't tell anyone, though. It's a secret."

Emily struggled to keep a straight face. "I won't. I appreciate you telling me. I know that would work with Sapphire. He loves ice cream."

They both turned to look at Sapphire, whose ears had perked up at the mention of ice cream. Caitlyn nodded. "I agree. He's definitely the ice cream type." She patted his head, which he'd politely lowered so she could reach him. "That's why he was bad for Alison at the show. Alison would never give him ice cream."

"That's why," Emily agreed.

Caitlyn cocked her head. "So how come you didn't ride Sapphire in the show?"

Emily resisted the urge to tell Caitlyn how annoying her mom was. Kyle might understand, but she wasn't about to make Caitlyn feel bad. "Um, his leg was still a little sore from last week."

Caitlyn frowned, then suddenly her face cleared and she nodded. "From when you took him without permission and got lost in the woods and fell off and they had to send out a team to rescue you? From then?"

Emily cleared her throat. "Um, yeah."

"So, really, it's because you're in trouble with my mom and she won't let you, right?"

Emily laughed at the knowing expression on Caitlyn's face. "Okay, you got me. That's part of it, yes."

Caitlyn nodded and leaned forward, lowering her voice. "The ice cream thing doesn't work with my mom."

"No? Too bad. I was about to try it."

"But tears do." Caitlyn gave a serious nod.

Emily raised her brows, surprised that even Caitlyn understood her mom was demanding. "Tears work on your mom? Seriously? But she's . . . so tough."

Caitlyn shrugged. "I'm just saying. Tears work." Then Caitlyn smacked her hand to the side of her head. "Oh, I forgot. I'm having a party in the hay barn tomorrow afternoon. I'm inviting my friend Tanya and you. Can you come?"

Emily couldn't help but be amused by the earnestness on Caitlyn's face. She might be only seven, but she was Emily's friend. "I'll come."

"Really? That's awesome! Make sure you dress up. It's a fancy party."

"Fancy? What kind of fancy?"

But Caitlyn was already skipping around the corner, singing a song about horses and beach balls that Emily was quite certain Caitlyn had invented.

Sapphire craned his head to watch Caitlyn as she darted out of sight, then he snorted and gave Emily a gentle shove with his nose, not enough to hurt her back.

She grinned and patted him. "Yeah, I agree. Let's keep her. She's okay." Her happiness faded as she saw Kyle pass by the end of the aisle and she remembered his comment. Was she really afraid?

Yeah.

She kind of was, and despite her claim to the contrary, she really didn't want to ride Moondance over fences tomorrow.

And that scared her even more. Horses were her life. She couldn't afford to be afraid of them. She looked at Sapphire. "I'm going to take that jumping lesson tomorrow and prove it. You think I should?"

He stomped his foot and nodded his head.

She wrinkled her nose at him. "I was hoping you were going to say no."

By the time Emily made it out to the barn the next morning, she was shaking.

Literally.

She lifted her arm to grab Moondance's bridle off the wall, and her hand was trembling so much she dropped the bridle. The metal bit clanged on the cement floor, and Emily stopped and leaned her forehead against the cool wood of the wall.

She closed her eyes, trying to calm her pounding heart while trickles of sweat ran down her spine. Tried to clear her mind, but all she could think about was that moment when Moondance tripped on the jump and she went over her head. When she'd landed. The pain. Not being able to move. Being packed off in the ambulance . . .

Then she thought of Kyle and his comments, and she stiffened. *I can do this.*

Emily wiggled her shoulders, did a quick jog in place to get her energy going, then she grabbed Moondance's bridle off the floor. She swept the saddle under her arm, resting it against her hip, and marched out the door toward Moondance's stall, taking a quick detour to greet Sapphire.

His black head peeked out at her. "I wish I was riding you," she whispered.

He snorted impatiently.

"I know. Soon, right?" Soon, ha. Aunt Debby would never let Emily ride him, and they both knew it. Sapphire was too precious and Emily was too . . . bad.

There. She'd admitted it. She was too bad.

Emily frowned, not liking the sound of the truth. She'd never liked being bad, and she still wasn't a fan. There was only one solution, and that was to get better.

Which meant she had to ride. As long as she focused on her goal of becoming the best rider Running Horse Ridge had ever produced, she could ignore the fear.

Hopefully.

She gave Sapphire a brisk pat, wanting to hurry off before she lost her determination. "I'll see you later. I have to go ride Moondance."

She rushed down the aisle, pausing to take one last glance over her shoulder at Sapphire. He was watching her, his ears perked forward, his brown eyes so cheerful that a little bit of the panic eased from her chest.

She knew he was waiting for her. Waiting for the time she'd come to his stall with tack to ride him.

Emily clenched her fists with renewed determination. Sapphire had faith in her. She couldn't let him down.

Twenty minutes later Emily had warmed up Moondance and was ready to jump. The gray mare had been in a playful mood, and it was making Emily a little bit nervous. Moondance was spooked by something in the bushes next to the cross-rail jump, and the mare did a little shimmy and a side step each time Emily rode her past it. Was it a shadow or a bird or the horse's imagination?

Emily didn't know, but all she could think about was what would happen if Moondance shied right when she was taking off over the jump? Would they crash again? Would they—

"So, are you all warmed up?"

Emily glanced over as Aunt Debby slid between the fence rails and walked into the ring. She was wearing jeans and paddock boots, and her hair was pulled off her face in a red bandanna. "Um, yeah."

"Great." Aunt Debby walked over to Emily and checked Moondance's girth, then set her hand on Emily's knee and peered up at her. "How are you doing?"

Emily shifted under her aunt's intense scrutiny. "Um, fine."

Aunt Debby narrowed her eyes for a moment, then gave Emily's leg a quick pat. "Okay, then. Go trot the cross rail."

Emily nodded, shortened her reins, then kicked Moondance into a trot. They passed by the cross bar, and Moondance raised her head, studying the bushes, then suddenly leaped sideways, cracking Emily's calf against the edge of the jump. She immediately reined in and looked at her aunt. "There's something in the bushes that's bothering Moondance today."

Aunt Debby shrugged. "You can handle it. Go ahead."

Go ahead. Emily took a deep breath, then nudged Moondance into a trot, taking the long way around the ring. Three days ago her aunt saying "you can handle it" would have made her feel great, but now she wasn't so sure her aunt was right. After Aunt Debby had been so casual about leaving Emily at the hospital, Emily was no longer certain she could trust her aunt's judgment.

"Emily? You're not even looking at the jump."

Emily turned her head and peeked at the cross rail, the red and white stripes so bright in the morning sun. She swallowed and plotted out her approach to it. All she had to do was turn and ride straight toward it. . . .

She turned and headed for it. Moondance raised her head and her ears went forward, and Emily knew she was looking at the bushes and not the jump and she was going to shy right when she was taking off and—

Moondance's body tensed to take off, then Emily jerked Moondance's head to the side to avoid the jump, forcing Moondance to take a sharp turn to keep from crashing into the jump standard.

"Emily? What was that?"

"Didn't like my approach," Emily mumbled. She took one hand off the reins and wiped it on her chaps. Her hands were so sweaty that she could barely hold the leather. Why hadn't she remembered her riding gloves this morning? She always rode with gloves. What if she lost her grip on the reins right when Moondance was taking off? "Do you have any gloves? I forgot mine."

"Emily." Aunt Debby was sounding impatient now. "You can manage without gloves for one lesson. Trot the jump."

"Yeah, okay." Emily took the long way around again, and ignored her aunt's request to cut across the ring.

She turned Moondance toward the jump and once again, Moondance's head went up and Emily knew the mare was going to shy. The jump was the same color as the one she'd fallen on at the show, and—

Emily hauled Moondance to a stop at the last second. The mare crashed into the jump and tripped on the rails, pulling down the cross rail as she stopped halfway over the jump, the rails rolling between her feet.

"Emily? Why did you stop?"

Emily threw her leg over Moondance and slid off, her legs shaking so much they almost gave out when her feet hit the ground. "I can't do it." Her voice was wavering and tears stung her eyes. "My back still hurts. The jarring"—she swallowed at the piercing look on her aunt's face—"hurts."

"Emily."

Emily didn't look at her aunt. Instead, she loosened Moondance's girth and tucked the stirrups up and out of the way so they didn't catch on anything on the way back into the barn. "So I'll put her away for now. I think I need another week or so. Plus my ankle still hurts. Yeah, that hurts, too. I need some more time. Wouldn't want to cause any permanent damage, you know?"

"Emily—"

"That's okay; it gives me more time to work with Hercules, right? And he needs help. So I'll see you later." Emily grabbed the reins and headed out of the ring, her cheeks flaming with humiliation, her legs still shaking.

"Emily!"

Emily finally turned back to look at her aunt. "What?"

"What is going on with you?"

Emily shook her head. "I'm just so bummed out that my back hurts. I'm really upset because I wanted to prove that the show was a fluke. That I can do it."

Aunt Debby studied her for a moment then nodded. "I understand. Go ahead. We'll try again later in the week."

She'd bought it? Emily mumbled her appreciation, then turned and hustled Moondance back toward the barn, glad she'd escaped without her aunt realizing the truth: that she was terrified of jumping and would never, ever be able to do it again.

It was over for her.

By the time Emily reached the back paddock with Sapphire in tow, she had made a decision: It didn't matter if she never jumped again.

She was a dressage rider. Dressage riders didn't jump. Everything was fine.

It was better than fine because she was no longer trying to be something she wasn't.

But as she passed by the trailer with the leftover jumps again, she couldn't deny the pit in her stomach. An aching, empty feeling like someone had dumped a load of rocks in there and then added a truckload of cement.

She wanted it to go away. Just go away and leave

her alone. Why was it bothering her so much? Why couldn't she shake it and move on?

Very frustrating!

Then she saw Hercules catch sight of them and whirl and sprint to the other side of the paddock, and she forgot about her own problems. "Hercules, sweetie. Good morning!

"I know you want me to go away, Hercules." Emily unhooked the gate and opened it wide, and Max lifted his head from the hay he'd been eating and whickered a greeting. "But I'm not going to leave you alone, because your life will be so much better if you have people in it, even if you're afraid of us right now, and even if you've convinced yourself you don't need people."

Hercules ran over to Max and snuggled against him while Sapphire studied the pair with great interest. "Okay, let's go get Max, Sapphire."

Emily walked up to Max, keeping Sapphire between herself and Hercules, and the little pony didn't bolt. He was watching her carefully, but he didn't take off. "See? I'm not so scary, am I? Whatever bad thing happened before won't happen again, I promise. It's all good from here on out." Emily hooked the lead shank to Max's halter, and then began to lead Sapphire and Max toward the gate. "Come along, Hercules. It'll be fun."

But he stood in the paddock and didn't follow them, even when they all walked out and began to walk down the path. He looked so scared and lonely standing there by himself, she almost went back and shut Max in the paddock with him.

She stopped and faced Hercules. "Come *on*, Hercules. You can't spend your life hiding back here, not when there's so much good stuff at the barn. Just follow Max. You can trust him, right?"

Hercules softly blew air out of his nose, and he didn't take a step toward them.

"Okay, fine, but you're going to miss a great party." She forced herself to turn away, then whispered to Max. "Tell him to come with us."

Max looked back at the ring and gave a loud whinny.

Hercules lifted his head, his ears forward.

Then Sapphire whickered, too, both horses gazing back at the pony.

Emily held her breath as Hercules took a small step toward them.

Then another.

And another.

And then Hercules was galloping after them, his little feet pounding in the dirt as he sprinted through the open gate and charged up toward them. He skidded to a stop next to Max, his ribs heaving and his nostrils flared. "Well, it's about time. Come on, we're going on a field trip."

She kept up a steady stream of chatter as she led the trio down toward the barn, Hercules moving closer and closer to Max's side the closer they got to the barn and all the activity.

And all the people.

She saw Kyle hauling a wheelbarrow into the main barn and quickly changed direction, knowing that Hercules would never tolerate Kyle's in-your-face manner. But Max's stall was in the main aisle where all the action was. . . .

She looked at Sapphire. "Can we borrow your stall?"

Sapphire immediately swung to the right and led the way toward the side entrance, the one nearest his stall. She led her trio into the side door, Hercules wedged so tightly against Max that their sides were bumping as they tried to walk.

But when she opened Sapphire's stall door and sent Max inside, there was a springiness to the old guy's step that hadn't been there before. His gray ears were up, his tail was swishing, and even his back seemed less swayed.

Hercules hurried after him, and Emily shut the door behind them.

She and Sapphire leaned over the door, watching as the two horses made themselves comfortable. To her surprise, Hercules seemed perfectly at ease in the large stall and didn't appear to feel trapped.

For now.

She had a feeling it would change the minute someone tried to enter his stall.

"Em?"

She looked up to see her aunt coming down the aisle. "Hercules is in here. He was perfectly happy to follow Max inside."

"Good work." Her aunt patted Sapphire as she peered inside the stall. Hercules startled at the sound of the new voice, then he scurried around to the other side of Max, hiding.

Aunt Debby was quiet for a moment, studying Hercules, then she carefully eased the stall door open and slid inside. "Keep talking to him, Emily, since he knows your voice."

Emily leaned on the door again, tugging Sapphire over so his head was leaning into the stall as well. "Hey, Hercules, this is my aunt Debby. She takes really good care of . . . her horses."

Aunt Debby glanced over at her, no doubt catching the hesitation in Emily's voice, so Emily rushed onward. "I mean, she's nice to horses, so you can trust her." Again, she couldn't quite keep the bitterness out of her tone, and she knew her aunt caught it by the long look she gave her.

But then her aunt walked around Max, and Hercules skittered around Max's rear end, reappearing on the side near Emily and away from Aunt Debby. Aunt Debby walked around Max again, crooning softly to Hercules, using a gentle tone Emily had never heard her aunt use.

Not that Hercules was fooled.

He kept just out of Aunt Debby's reach no matter how she tried to approach him, and he was sweating and trembling, his coat caked with wetness, his flanks shaking so badly, Emily could see it from the door.

After about fifteen minutes, Aunt Debby looked at Emily. "Get me a lead shank."

Emily grabbed one off Sapphire's door. "Don't you think it'll scare Hercules if you tie him up?"

Aunt Debby grimaced. "I'm afraid so, but I have to give him a quick once over to make sure he's all right. Hopefully, it won't set him back too far."

This time, when Hercules tried to dodge her,

Aunt Debby slid the lead shank around his neck and anchored him. Hercules stopped instantly, not fighting the restraints, as if he knew he was caught.

But his eyes were rolled back, his body was shaking, and he looked like he was going to collapse. "Oh, Hercules!" Emily opened the door to go in, and stopped when Aunt Debby held up her hand.

"More people will make Hercules worse." Aunt Debby's voice was soft, so quiet Emily barely heard it. "Just talk to him from there."

Max nickered softly and moved closer to Hercules, and Sapphire stretched his head over the gate toward Hercules.

But still the little pony continued to shake, and the moment Aunt Debby touched his fetlock, he jerked back in terror, his body slamming into Max's side. "It's okay, Hercules," Aunt Debby crooned as she followed him, quickly running her hands over his legs. She kept talking to him as she picked up each foot, inspecting it.

Emily couldn't believe how gentle her aunt was being. She was like . . . like a mom. Like a mom should be. So warm and loving and kind. It made her throat tighten to see her aunt comforting Hercules, giving him only love as she efficiently checked him out, moving quickly to spare him prolonged torture, but still so gentle and reassuring in her movements.

Emily leaned forward, falling under her aunt's spell, letting the wonderful sensations her aunt was creating coat her in warmth. She'd never seen anyone be as comforting as her aunt was being; never had anyone used that tone with her, even on her worst days. "Why didn't you treat me like that when I fell off Moondance?"

Her aunt looked up from where she was massaging the left rear ankle of Hercules. "What are you talking about?"

"You're so . . ." Emily felt her cheeks begin to heat up, and she stopped. What was she going to do? Beg her aunt to treat her like a horse? Yikes. "How is Hercules?"

Aunt Debby studied her for another moment, and Emily thought that maybe her aunt was going to force Emily to continue with what she was going to say. But instead Aunt Debby patted Hercules's rump and stood up. "He's not too bad. He could use some work on his feet, and his ankle is a little swollen, but nothing we have to treat right now." Her aunt eased her way out of the stall, her movements subtle and slow so as not to panic the pony. "At this point, I think the best thing for him is time."

Emily opened the door as Aunt Debby stepped out.

"So, are you going to take over his care from me?"

Aunt Debby cocked her head as she closed the door. "I need to think about the best approach. I'll let you know."

"Yeah, sure." Emily knew she wouldn't be trusted with him, and that totally bugged her. She already loved him and knew he needed someone who truly cared.

Then again, her aunt had been incredibly nice to him, so maybe Emily *wasn't* the best one. Maybe Aunt Debby was right about all of it!—riding Sapphire, training T.J., taking care of Hercules. . . .

Emily sighed. She was so confused. She didn't know what she was capable of, what she wasn't, what to do next. . . .

"Will you take Hercules and Max back to the paddock?" Aunt Debby asked, giving Emily a thoughtful look, as if she were reading Emily's mind.

"Yeah, sure." Emily opened the door and walked inside, hooking Max back up as Hercules scrambled around to the other side. But when she turned to walk back, she saw her aunt looking at her strangely. "What?"

"You're moving well."

"What do you mean?"

"You aren't acting like your back hurts."

"Oh. *Oh.*" Emily touched her back, which she'd actually forgotten about. "It, um, only hurts when I jump."

"Huh." Aunt Debby gave her another long look, then turned and walked off.

And Emily didn't like the fact at all that she couldn't read Aunt Debby's expression. Aunt Debby had an agenda, Emily was sure, and Emily had a feeling she wasn't going to like it.

Scott Summers found his sister sitting in the kitchen later that night. Everyone else had gone to bed, and Debby was still up. He pulled out a chair and sat down across from her. "Got a minute?"

Debby looked up from the laptop computer she'd been typing on. Scott realized how tired she was, and stressed, and he was glad he'd decided to stay at the farm for a while and help get it back into shape. But only if staying worked for Emily.

"Sure. What's going on?" Debby asked.

"It's Emily."

Debby's face stiffened ever so slightly. "What about her?"

"I think . . ." He paused, trying to figure out the best way to express his concerns. "I know you've really gone out of your way to welcome her to the farm and get her involved, but I think it's not going very well."

Debby sighed and sat back in her chair, looking ever more tired. "I know. She made some comments today that . . ." She shook her head. "Do you think it's that I left her at the hospital?"

"Among other things." Scott leaned forward. "I think we made a mistake with that decision. None of the kids should ever be left alone in the hospital." He couldn't keep the tension out of his voice. "Horses don't come first sometimes."

He expected argument, but Debby nodded. "I know. I made a mistake." She sighed. "But that's not all it is, is it?"

Scott shook his head, relieved that Debby had agreed with him. He could tell from her tone that she did regret it and that it wouldn't happen again. "I think Emily feels like she's losing me. She's not feeling part of things here."

Debby shut her computer and gave Scott her full focus. "I tried to get her back in the ring, but she's not interested. I don't know what to do. I can't teach her dressage, and if that's what she needs—"

"No." Scott rubbed his jaw. "I think . . . I think she needs to feel like she belongs. She needs to believe that this is her family and her farm as much as it is mine."

Debby studied him. "It would have been a lot easier if you'd brought her back to see us before this."

Scott ground his jaw against the guilt that Debby's statement brought up. He had enough issues around coming back, and he wasn't going to get into them with his sister. This discussion was about Emily. "What do you think about a trail ride and picnic? Like the old days?"

Debby raised her brows. "I haven't thought of those trail rides in forever. We don't have time to take a whole day off—"

"We need to make time." Scott nodded, growing more certain the longer he thought about it. "For all of us." He met his sister's eyes. "I'm not going anywhere, Debby, and it's equally as important for you and me to connect as well. You with Emily, me with your kids and Rick, and Emily with everyone."

Debby looked at her computer, and Scott knew she was thinking about all the work that had to be done.

"It'll all still be there if you take a day off." He leaned forward. "I'm going to take Emily tomorrow, and anyone else who will come. I hope you join us."

When Debby didn't say anything, he pushed back

from the table to head upstairs and tell Emily about the plan if she was still awake. It was so late, he doubted she was. He'd reached the doorway when his sister said his name.

"Scott?"

He turned back. "Yes?"

She gave him a weary smile that had a hint of cautious hope. "We'll all go on the trail ride tomorrow."

Scott grinned back, suddenly feeling like he was fifteen again, eagerly anticipating a day out on the trails.

Then he thought of Emily's sad eyes and the betrayal in them when he'd told her what he'd done with Rhapsody's lease, and some of his confidence faded. It was what Emily needed, but would it be enough?

Emily walked into the kitchen the next morning to find Meredith and Caitlyn making sandwiches. There were an assortment of leather saddle bags with straps on the table, cans of soda, and a pan of freshly baked brownies on the counter. The smell of chocolate hit Emily the moment she pushed open the door, and her mouth started watering even before she saw the pan of brownies. "What's going on?"

"Trail ride today," Meredith announced. "Caitlyn and I are finishing up the food. Everyone is rushing through the barn chores so we can get out of here." She tossed a plastic container at Emily. "Will you put the brownies in here?"

"A trail ride?" Emily caught the container. "Who's going?"

"The family," Caitlyn said. "Plus Meredith because she's like family." Caitlyn grabbed a big bag of potato chips and jammed them into one of the leather bags.

"Oh." The family? The last thing Emily needed was to spend the day with people who didn't want her along. "I don't think I can go. My back—"

"No!" Meredith interrupted before Emily could even give her excuse. She waved a carrot at Emily. "You have to go. It's going to be so fun!"

"Yeah!" Caitlyn came to stand behind Meredith, her hands on her hips as she chomped on a potato chip she'd just swiped. "You promised to come to my party in the hay barn today, and I'm doing this instead. So you already said you'd come!"

Emily stared at Caitlyn and Meredith and realized they weren't faking it. They really wanted her to come. Like, *really*. She nodded. "I guess I'll come, then."

"Woohoo!" Meredith threw up her hand and slapped Caitlyn a high five, then they both high-fived Emily. Twice.

Emily started laughing when Caitlyn went back for a third high five. "You guys need help or what?"

"Of course!" Meredith handed Emily a butter knife. "Dish up those brownies, girl! We're on a deadline! And give me one of them before you pack them up. I can't possibly wait all day for chocolate."

"Me either!"

Emily hummed cheerfully as she cut the brownies, handing one over to each of the others and keeping one for herself before filling up the plastic container. Caitlyn and Meredith rushed around the kitchen at a frenzied pace, shoving food in their mouths as fast as they were packing it in the saddle bags.

Caitlyn held up a small plastic container she'd pulled out of the fridge. "Salmon paste for the crackers." She wrinkled her nose. "Yes or no?"

The three of them looked at one another, then they all shouted "No!" at the same time, promptly descending into hysteria as Caitlyn pulled off the top and set it on the counter under Max's window for him to munch on next time he showed up.

Emily grinned at Meredith as she began to pack the pickles in a plastic bag, suddenly very much looking forward to the day. So what if her family was going to be there? She'd have fun anyway!

They were about two hours into the trail ride, surrounded by thick woods and lush vegetation that smelled like damp springtime. Emily had fallen behind the others, enjoying the bonding but a little tired of trying to explain why she wasn't jumping, of retelling the story about her disastrous show. Of course, the gang was also giving Alison a hard time for her horrible model class with Sapphire, but Alison didn't seem to mind. Emily did. She just wasn't used to a family getting all in her business the way this one did.

Plus, both Meredith and Alison were riding their own beautiful horses, and Emily just felt . . . plain, riding Moondance.

Sapphire hadn't been permitted to come on the trail ride because he was too unpredictable. Aunt Debby was afraid whoever rode him would fall off and he'd get away.

Emily missed him. A lot.

She knew Aunt Debby was probably right that Sapphire would misbehave, but she didn't care. It wasn't the same without him.

"Em?"

She glanced over at her dad, who was riding a huge, dark bay horse named Spartacus. The horse was spirited and energetic, and her dad had had his hands full for the first two hours. Emily was actually impressed with her dad's skills. She hadn't realized how talented he was at riding. "You're good."

Her dad looked pleased. "Starting to get the feel back again." He patted Spartacus's muscular neck. "I didn't realize how much I missed it." He slanted a look at Emily. "Had I realized, I would have been right there beside you at the barn, taking lessons."

She snorted. "Dressage? You think dressage is worthless."

He raised his brows. "Do I?"

She looked at him and suddenly thought of the thousands of hours he'd spent at horse shows with her.

Of all the money he'd spent on leasing the best horses for her. Of the countless times he'd listened to her rant about a show or a lesson or a horse. Never once had he even mentioned his other life as a hunter/jumper rider. Never once had he suggested she try jumping instead of dressage.

Emily's dad patted her leg, his face softening. "Emily, I think dressage is great, and I think you're a fantastic rider. In fact, dressage is very difficult, and I know that if I was going to learn dressage, I'd have to start at the bottom, because there are so many things I never learned as a hunter/jumper rider."

"Oh, totally! There's so much . . ." Her voice faded as she realized what her dad had said. What his point was. "You're saying that I shouldn't be embarrassed to be starting over with the jumping?"

He nodded. "Jumping is different. The whole world is different. But you'll catch on so fast, as long as you give yourself a break." He leaned closer to her. "I love you, Em."

She looked at her dad then, saw the sincerity on his face. "Then why—"

"We're here because I think it'll be best for you. Do you think it's easy for me to walk away from my life in New Jersey? I had friends there, too. I'm doing my business from here, but it's not the same thing. I feel like this is important. *Family* is important, and it's time you had a solid support system around you. I'm doing this for you, Emily." He gestured toward the mountains in the distance. "Isn't it wonderful? Doesn't it do something for you?"

She looked around her, at the trees surrounding her, at the row of horses in front of her. Meredith turned around in the saddle and grinned at her, and Emily waved back then looked at her dad, who watched them with a pleased expression on his face.

"When was the last time you got to spend the day with me *and* horses?" he asked. "I'm so glad I can share this with you now."

She gave a slight nod. He had a point.

She patted Moondance's neck then gaped as Aunt Debby let out a whoop up front and kicked her horse into a canter. Everyone else leaped forward, including Moondance. Emily rose into a half-seat, giving Moondance loose reins as they galloped along the wooded path, eight sets of hooves thudding on the dirt.

Uncle Rick shouted something she couldn't understand, but suddenly her aunt and cousins starting singing. A rowdy song she didn't know about the old

west and riding the trails. But everyone was screaming it, including her dad, and suddenly Emily started
laughing. "You guys are crazy!"

"You had no idea, did you?" her dad shouted back,
urging Spartacus along. His hair was whipping in the
wind; he was laughing—laughing like she'd never seen
him laugh.

"Les would kill you for encouraging me to ride this
recklessly!" she shouted at him.

Her dad rolled his eyes. "Les doesn't know what he's
missing! This is what riding is all about!" He clucked to
Spartacus and moved ahead, yelling to his sister that he
was going to beat her.

And then next thing Emily knew, her dad and her
aunt were tearing down the path side-by-side, battling
each other. Her dad? Drag racing on horseback through
the woods? And Aunt Debby, too? Emily had had no
idea they'd ever do something like that. Something just
for fun. How completely crazy.

And she realized then that her dad was absolutely
right. It wasn't about dressage. It wasn't even about
jumping. It was about galloping through the woods,
yelling and shouting, ducking under branches, being
completely free and wild and . . . crazy!

Then suddenly she saw a series of downed logs across

the trail ahead, and Uncle Rick's horse flew over the first one, and then two more in quick succession. Then Aunt Debby jumped, and then Caitlyn hopped over them on her pony, then Alison—

Emily sat up and hauled Moondance back, the mare fighting her hard because she wanted to follow her friends. Meredith glanced back over her shoulder, then immediately slowed Halo, coming to a stop beside Emily as the others continued to ride over the logs. "What's wrong?"

"I can't do it." Emily's heart was pounding, her chest tight, her throat dry, and she struggled to get Moondance to stop.

"Can't what?"

Emily shook her head frantically, already starting to sweat. "I can't do it. I can't jump," she whispered.

Meredith frowned. "Why not?"

Emily shot a glance at her, her hands already starting to shake. "I'm scared," she whispered. "I'm so scared."

Meredith's face cleared in understanding just as Aunt Debby hollered for them to hurry up.

Meredith turned to her aunt. "Emily has never gone off-roading!" she shouted back. "We'll catch up." She turned Halo to the right, and her horse stepped off the trail and into the bushes. "Come on, Em."

Emily directed Moondance into the woods behind Halo and Meredith. "We're going around the trees?"

Meredith nodded. "We're going around the trees."

Emily clucked Moondance to catch up so she was riding beside Meredith. "Thanks for saving me," she whispered. "You're too awesome."

"You should tell them you're scared."

"No, I can't. They'll think I'm an idiot."

"Do I?"

Emily frowned. "You don't seem to . . . but I didn't mean to tell you. I just didn't know what else to do."

Meredith shook her head as the horses picked their way through the woods. "Emily, you've got it wrong. Debby seems tough, but she's been in the horse business for a long, long time. She'd totally understand."

"No, trust me. She wouldn't. She already thinks I'm incompetent. If she also thought I was scared, then—"

Meredith interrupted. "When I first got Halo, he was really bad in the stall. He was a biter."

Emily ducked under a low pine branch. "So?"

"So he bit me six times the first day. I had terrible bruises on my side and my shoulder, and he nearly crushed my fingers." Meredith wove Halo around a low pine tree.

"Really? He seems so nice."

Meredith looked at Emily. "After that first day I walked into the ring where Debby was giving Alison a lesson and I announced I was giving him back."

Emily raised her brows. "Really?"

Meredith looked at her, then got thonked by a branch. She pressed her hand to her head while Emily ducked. "Yes. I told her he was a monster, and if I kept him, he was going to eat me alive, and I was never going near him again. Ever."

"What did she say?" Emily glanced at the root system of the first downed tree. It looked pretty big from that angle.

Meredith tightened her grip on Halo's reins as he slogged through a small stream. "She asked me if I was afraid of him."

Emily followed Halo through the water, keeping a tight grip in case Moondance decided to jump the stream like Sapphire had done when she'd been on the joyride with him. But Moondance picked her way across the wet stones carefully and delicately, like a lady. "What did you say?" They passed the second downed tree, and it actually looked pretty small. Moondance could have stepped over it at a walk.

Meredith looked back. "I told Debby that I wasn't just afraid of Halo. I told her he was an evil demon horse that would haunt me for the rest of my life."

Emily burst out laughing. "You didn't!"

"I totally did. I needed her to understand exactly how bad the situation was." Meredith wrinkled her nose. "So Debby told me that she would work with me and help me deal with the situation. And she did. She went with me into Halo's stall every single time for the next three weeks. And if she couldn't do it, Alison went with me. Never once did either of them pressure me to face him alone."

Emily bit her lip as they passed the final downed tree. "Seriously?"

"Seriously." Meredith turned Halo back toward the path, where the rest of the group was almost out of sight down the trail. "You should trust them, Em. I'm sure Debby would be able to help. She seems tough, but she cares. She really does."

"About the horses."

Meredith kicked Halo into a trot. "She cares about us, too."

Emily bit her lip, realizing that a part of her really, *really* wished Meredith was right. She looked up ahead and saw her aunt riding next to Alison, their heads bent in discussion, and she knew she wanted that to be her. She wanted to be part of that group. *So badly.* Would admitting she was scared make that happen? Or would it be the final blow to any chance she had at belonging? She wanted them to respect her so much.

As she looked around at the people she was with, at the beautiful woods, as she listened to the laughter and the songs, she realized that she wanted to belong here.

She really, truly did.

By the time the farm came into view eight hours later, Emily was exhausted. And delirious with excitement. And more depressed than she could ever remember being.

It had been the most amazing day. Hours of riding, the picnic lunch on the edge of a beautiful pond, the laughter, the jokes . . . Everyone was so nice and so happy and . . . fun.

She'd never seen that fun side of her dad or her aunt and uncle before. And she loved it. She'd truly never had as much fun with horses as she had all day.

"Have a good day, Em?"

Emily grinned as Aunt Debby rode up beside her. "It

was fantastic! Thanks so much for letting me come."

"For letting you come?" Aunt Debby laughed. "Emily, you're part of the family. You aren't allowed to miss these kinds of things."

Emily felt all warm and giddy. "Really?"

"Really." Aunt Debby cocked her head. "I noticed that you rode around all the jumps today. Your back still bothering you?"

Emily hesitated, thinking of Meredith's words. What if Aunt Debby could help her? She opened her mouth to tell the truth, then had a sudden vision of Aunt Debby's face turning away in disappointment. Of all the magic of today disappearing when Aunt Debby found out the truth about her: that Emily really and truly wasn't capable of handling the jumping. Jumping was the soul of Running Horse Ridge, and if Emily couldn't handle it, what place would there be for her?

Alison rode up beside them on Icy. "This was a fantastic day, Mom. Thanks for organizing."

Aunt Debby nodded but didn't take her gaze off Emily, clearly waiting for an answer.

Alison glanced at Emily. "What's going on, cuz? Is my mom giving you grief? If she is, tell me and I'll ride interference. No grief-giving is allowed on field trip day."

Emily blinked, staring at Alison. "You'd defend me?"

"Of course I would." Alison grinned. "We have to team up to save ourselves from her, you know."

Emily smiled at the affection in Alison's voice, at the teasing. She felt like she belonged. Like she really did.

After such a fun day, Emily couldn't handle going back to worrying what they were thinking about her, to fearing that they didn't respect her. Which meant she couldn't tell them the truth. "My back still hurts, yes," she lied. "I can't do the lesson tomorrow. Sorry."

Aunt Debby gave her a long look while Alison tapped Emily's leg. "Race you back to the barn, cuz."

Emily jumped on the chance to get away from Aunt Debby's scrutiny. "You're on!" She kicked Moondance into a gallop, and her mount leaped ahead of Icy and Alison.

"No racing after such a long day," Aunt Debby called out. "Keep it slow!"

"Hey!" Alison dug hard to catch up, and Emily laughed as Meredith shouted something and set Halo after them.

None of them were riding hard with Aunt Debby keeping an eye on them, but Emily felt great to let

Moondance's head go and feel the wind whipping across her face, to laugh with Meredith and Alison, just to have fun!

They cantered past Hercules's pasture, and Emily reined up to check on him. But the pasture was empty, and the gate was open. Emily frowned and looked around. Had he gotten out or had one of the temporary extra help moved him?

Alison and Meredith pulled up. "What's wrong?" Meredith asked.

"Hercules. He's missing." Emily clucked Moondance forward, starting to worry. What if someone had pulled him out of the ring and had him locked down somewhere, terrifying him?

"Hercules?" Alison frowned. "Who is that?"

"A Shetland pony I was working with. Aunt Debby!" Emily flagged down her aunt as she approached, distantly trailed by the rest of the group. "Hercules is missing. Do you know where he is?"

Aunt Debby's relaxed face snapped into tense concern. "No one should have touched him. He must have gotten out—"

There was the pounding of hooves and they all turned to see Sapphire galloping toward them. He was wearing his halter, the lead shank trailing behind him.

Emily grinned. "Sapphire missed me!"

Sure enough, Sapphire pounded right up to them, skidding to a stop as Moondance shied to the left to keep from getting plowed. Sapphire nickered at Emily, prancing in place.

"Well, now we know how Hercules got out," Alison said. "Sapphire got out and then opened the paddock gate. We need to make all the locks on this farm Sapphire-proof." She sidled up and tried to grab Sapphire's lead shank, but he danced out of the way, keeping out of reach.

Emily snapped her fingers. "Sapphire! Come here." She couldn't help but smile when he marched right up to her and thrust his face over Moondance's withers, giving Emily easy access to his lead shank. She quickly grabbed it, giving him a big kiss on his nose.

"He so loves you." Meredith sighed. "That is too cool."

"I love him." Emily scratched his ears, trying not to look at her aunt, knowing that she still had plans to sell Sapphire.

But before she could snuggle too much, Sapphire pulled his head back and stared up at the woods behind the house. Emily tugged on his lead shank. "Come on, Sapphire, we're going to the barn."

Sapphire shook his head and stomped his foot, still focused on the woods, his ears too alert. Then Moondance lifted her head and was staring in the same direction as Sapphire.

And so were Halo and Icy.

"What's over there?" Emily frowned and stood in her stirrups, trying to see what had caught the horses' attention, but there was only woods. She tightened her grip on Moondance's reins and Sapphire's lead shank. "You guys see anything?"

"No." Meredith shaded her eyes as Halo danced beneath her, straining to go up into the woods. All the horses were agitated, focused on the hillside. "Alison?"

"I don't either—"

"You guys hear that?" Aunt Debby rode up next to Moondance.

"Hear what?"

"Listen."

Emily and the other girls fell silent, watching the woods. For a moment, Emily heard nothing but the sounds of the horses shifting and breathing.

And then she heard it. The sound of a horse neighing. Again and again and again . . . Goose bumps popped up on Emily's arms. "Something's wrong—"

"That sounds like it's coming from the woods,"

Meredith said. "We don't have horses up there, do we?"

"No, we don't." Aunt Debby looked grim. "Let's go." She launched her horse into a canter, heading straight up the hillside, Meredith and Alison riding hard behind her.

Emily's stomach dropped as she hustled after Aunt Debby, remembering the empty paddock that Hercules was supposed to be in. The pony had suffered so much already. *Please let him be okay.*

They galloped around behind the house, then headed up into the woods, crashing through the underbrush, Sapphire charging alongside Emily as she held on to the lead shank. "How do you know where we're going?" she asked her aunt. "Shouldn't we stop and listen?"

Aunt Debby called back over her shoulder. "Grandpa had a shed up here that he used to come to when he wanted privacy. He and Max used to hang out there all the time. It's fallen down and—"

Emily gasped as they rounded the corner and she saw a half-collapsed pile of boards and shingles that used to be a cabin. Max was standing next to the pile, and the moment he saw them, he lifted his head and nickered. Emily realized it was his whinny they'd heard from the back pasture. She sighed with relief. "He looks okay—"

That's when she saw Hercules. The little pony was buried under the rubble up to his shoulders. All that was visible were his neck and head. His eyes were rimmed with white, his neck slathered with sweat. He was trapped!

"*H*ercules!" Aunt Debby vaulted off her horse and ran for the cabin, but the instant she got close, Hercules practically screamed in terror and he threw himself backward, trying to get away. Aunt Debby stopped dead as the shed shifted and moaned, and more boards fell on Hercules.

"Hercules," Aunt Debby crooned with surprising calmness. "I'm here to help you."

The pony continued to struggle and Emily gasped as what remained of the roof shifted. "It's going to fall on him!"

Aunt Debby quickly backed up, and the moment she did Hercules stopped struggling, but his ribs were heaving and his eyes were still wild.

"Emily." Aunt Debby's voice was quiet. "Come down here."

Emily quickly slid off Moondance and led Sapphire and Moondance up to Aunt Debby. Hercules's gaze jerked toward them as they approached. "What do you need?"

"If there's any chance of him trusting anyone, it'll be you. I need you to go up there and free him."

"Me?"

"Or at least keep him calm enough so I can do it." Aunt Debby pulled Moondance's reins and Sapphire's lead shank out of her hands and gave her an impatient push. "Go!"

Emily swallowed hard, not at all sure Hercules would trust her any more than he'd trusted Aunt Debby, but she knew she had no choice but to try. She eased forward, whispering to Hercules. "Hey, sweetie, you've got yourself in quite the difficult spot, haven't you?"

His ears went forward to listen to her, and his body tensed, but he didn't struggle. Yet.

She took another step forward. "So Sapphire and I are here to help you. See him behind me? You know Sapphire, remember?" Sapphire whickered behind her, and Hercules raised his head to look at him. "And Max is here, too. He trusts me, and you know you can trust his judgment." She reached Max, saw his front feet were on some boards, as he'd clearly gotten as close to Hercules as he could.

She patted Max's neck, and the old horse's ears were pinned back, and he was trembling. "Hey, Max, don't worry, sweetie. We're going to get your new friend out of there. You're not going to lose two best friends in the same summer, I promise."

She studied the little pony, saw the way he was trapped and how terrified he looked, and her heart started to pound. "I can't do this," she whispered. "What if I screw up and he gets even more badly hurt?" Emily's stomach roiled, and she knew she couldn't face the results if she messed up. She turned to tell her aunt she couldn't do it. "I can't—"

Then she saw Sapphire standing beside her aunt. His black head was held high, and he was watching the scene intently, his body vibrating with energy and adrenaline. Emily realized that Sapphire would never be afraid. He would plunge right in and do whatever he felt like doing. It's what he always did, and that was what she loved about him. He had no fear, no regrets, and his commitment to everything he did was absolute.

If Sapphire were in her situation, he wouldn't hesitate

for even a second. He pulled his gaze from Hercules and looked right at Emily. For a moment he stared at her, and then a new strength rose within her. A new courage. Sapphire's courage. Sapphire's spirit.

And she knew she could do this.

Emily gave Sapphire a nod, then turned back to Max and Hercules. She trailed her fingers over Max's nose, then moved past him, climbing carefully onto a pile of boards. She stopped when she was less than two feet from Hercules, and she saw the tremors in his body. He was terrified, beyond terrified . . . yet he wasn't trying to run. He was watching her and Max intently, his eyes so wide they looked like they were going to pop out of his head.

"Hey, sweetie." She eased closer as Max nickered softly and stretched his nose out toward Hercules. Hercules extended his neck, and they just barely managed to brush noses across the boards.

"Okay, so I won't try to touch you, but I'm going to pull some of these boards back, okay?" He was fixated on her now, watching every move as she reached toward his back.

She expected him to try to bolt, but he didn't move even a step as she grabbed a large board and tugged it toward her, still talking to him as Max watched closely, periodically whickering.

The board crashed to the ground with a loud pop. Hercules jumped, but he didn't struggle or try to run. He just kept his gaze fixed on Max, as if trying to shut out the fact Emily was so close.

"I think he's going to let me help him." She spoke loud enough for her aunt to hear.

"Good work, Emily." Her aunt's voice was so quiet that Emily barely heard it. But she *did* hear it, and she heard the tension and relief in her aunt's voice, and realized that everyone was counting on her. She was the only one who could help him. The only one he'd trust enough.

"Okay, Hercules, let's get you out of here." She moved more quickly now, realizing Hercules wasn't going to panic. She grabbed board after board, yanking it off him. And the little pony never once tried to move. His feet were planted firmly on the ground, his gaze plastered to Max. Hercules was still shaking, but his eyes weren't as wide as they had been when they arrived, and his ribs weren't heaving as much as they had been.

She squatted by his front feet and yanked a wooden beam out from between his hooves, realizing that as scared as Hercules was, her presence had eased some of his fear. He truly trusted her to make it better.

She ducked under his neck, patting him as she went beneath him, and he didn't flinch. "Almost done, sweetie."

Two more boards, and then he was free.

But still he didn't try to move. It was as if he was afraid to try.

So Emily walked in front of him and wound her fingers through his thick mane. "Come on, Hercules. All you need to do is step on some boards and you'll be out." She tugged gently on his mane, and Hercules stared at her.

Then he slowly lifted one tiny hoof and gingerly planted it on a sheet of plywood. "Good boy. Can you do it again?" She tugged gently, and Hercules took another step, never taking his eyes off Max.

Then he took one more, and another, and another, and suddenly he was out!

For a split second Hercules turned to look at Emily, and she gave him a thumbs-up. "You did it, Hercules!" She opened her arms to give him a hug, and he ducked out of her embrace and bolted past her.

But he whirled around to face her when he was only about five feet away, and he gave a shuddering sigh of relief as Max hurried over to him and started sniffing him.

Emily beamed as Aunt Debby walked up, leading Sapphire, Moondance, and the horse she'd been riding. Sapphire immediately rested his chin on Emily's shoulder, and she wrapped her arms around his nose, surprised to discover she was trembling. She sagged against him as her adrenaline left in a shaky rush, and suddenly all she wanted to do was collapse. "Thanks for being there for me," she whispered into his ear. "I couldn't have done it without you." Without Sapphire she knew she never would have had the courage to take the chance of failing.

Then Aunt Debby grabbed Emily in a giant hug. "You did it!"

Hercules startled and trotted away from them as Alison and Meredith let out a huge cheer. Emily grinned at them all, leaning against Aunt Debby as she threw her arm over Emily's shoulders and hauled her tight against her. "You did fantastic, Emily. You saved him."

Emily watched Max head toward the barn, Hercules tight on his tail. "He saved himself by realizing he needed to trust me."

"That he did." Aunt Debby squeezed her again and then dropped her arm. "Okay, everyone, let's head back." She glanced at Emily. "I want Uncle Rick to check out Hercules and make certain he's all right. Can you help him with that? You need to be there. I'll put Sapphire away—" She reached out for him, and Emily grabbed his halter first.

"I'll take him with me, if that's okay. I just—" She held up her hand, which was shaking visibly. "I just need him with me right now." She tensed, waiting for Aunt Debby to contradict her, to say she shouldn't be that dependent on him, but all Aunt Debby did was cock her head.

"You and Sapphire really have something special going on, don't you?"

Emily nodded. "Is that a problem?"

Aunt Debby sighed and tucked Emily's hair behind her ear. "No, Em, it isn't. I just don't want your heart to be broken when he leaves. That's all I'm trying to protect you from."

And Emily saw in her aunt's eyes the truth. They were soft and warm. Her aunt really did care about her. Truly. "I'm scared," she blurted out.

Aunt Debby frowned. "About losing Sapphire?"

"About jumping." Emily heard a horse snort, and she jerked her gaze to the right, realizing with horror that Alison and Meredith were still there, and they were listening. She dropped her gaze to her feet, kicking at a rock with her dusty paddock boots. "Never mind—"

"I refused to canter for two years when I first started to ride," Alison said.

Emily peeled her gaze off the forest floor. "What?"

"It terrified me. I refused." She rolled her eyes at herself. "I used to be a major wimp."

"Really?" Emily's shoulders relaxed.

Alison nodded. "Swear. And jumping? Forget it. I was having no part of it."

Aunt Debby chuckled and put her arm around Emily's shoulders again. "I'd pretty much given up turning Alison into a rider until she saw the summer Olympics on television and she fell in love with one of the horses. After watching him jump those huge jumps, the little cross rail didn't look so scary, and she was hooked."

"*Really?* You aren't making fun of me?"

"Heck no," Meredith said. "We're all scared at some point. You remember the demon pony?" she asked Emily's aunt.

Aunt Debby started to laugh. "I have to admit, Halo had me a little worried for a while. The reason I went in his stall with you was as much to protect you as to make you feel better. You trained him well."

Meredith patted Halo's neck with obvious affection. "Now he's a softie."

"A softie with teeth," Alison said. "You still can't turn your back on him."

Emily couldn't believe the banter. Even her aunt had been worried about Halo? "So you don't think I'm a loser?"

Aunt Debby led Emily across the clearing. "No, Emily, we don't. It makes total sense that you'd be scared." She squeezed Emily's shoulders again, then dropped her arm. "I think I know how to make you not scared anymore. Be at the ring at eight tomorrow morning."

Emily swallowed, her hands going clammy. "For a jumping lesson?"

Aunt Debby shook her head. "Just come to the ring ready to ride. Trust me."

"Trust you?" Emily looked at Aunt Debby. She was beaming at her, a smile that was supportive and kind, and Emily knew her aunt was on her side. So she took a deep breath and nodded. "Okay. I'll be there. I'll trust you."

And then her aunt got the biggest grin on her face that Emily had ever seen, and hugged Emily tightly. "Thank you for saying that, Emily." She pulled back and kissed Emily on the forehead, her eyes a little shinier than normal. "Thank you."

At three minutes after eight o'clock the next morning, Emily sat down on her bed. Fully dressed in her chaps, helmet, paddock boots, and riding gloves. Ready to ride.

But so not.

"I can't do this," she whispered. She held out her hands, not surprised to see them shaking.

There was a knock on the door, and before Emily could pull her hands back, the door opened, and her dad walked in. He was wearing a faded red T-shirt that he always wore for yard work in New Jersey, and she chuckled, remembering digging up weeds alongside of him many times.

He came in and sat down beside her, the bed creaking beneath his weight. "Hey, Em."

Emily looked up in surprise. "What are you doing here?"

"Aunt Debby told me about your conversation with her yesterday. That you were scared to jump. Thought you might be nervous about going down to the ring this morning, so I thought I'd walk you down there."

She took a deep breath and then looked at him. "Would you be disappointed in me if I didn't ever jump? I really don't know if I can."

He smiled and lightly rapped his knuckles on her helmet. "Emily, don't be silly. I stopped riding for more than ten years. If riding isn't right for you, then that's fine."

Tears filled her eyes. "Really? So I don't have to go down there?"

He caught her chin and forced her to look at him. "Walking away from riding because you're not interested in it is completely fine. But walking away from riding because you're scared, knowing that you still love it and would like to ride, is a huge mistake. Which is it, Emily?"

She blew out a puff of air, unable to lie. "I'm scared," she mumbled.

Her dad nodded. "Then the only answer is to go out there and climb on. Aunt Debby's not going to have you do anything that makes you nervous."

"But jumping makes me nervous!" As the words burst out of her mouth, Emily realized how good it felt to be able to say them freely. She even smiled, despite her shaking hands.

"Well, let's go see what Aunt Debby has planned before you make up your mind, okay?" He stood up and held out his hand. "Come on, Em. It'll be okay."

She took a deep breath, then stood up and grabbed her dad's hand. "Thanks for coming up to get me."

He smiled down at her as they walked out the door. "Anytime, Em. And if I ever forget to come get you when you need me to, don't hesitate to tell me, okay?"

She grinned at him. "I'll totally give you grief."

He winked. "Sounds perfect." They reached the top of the stairs. "After you, my dear."

And just like that, Emily's good feelings vanished, replaced by a trembling in her belly that reminded her of Hercules . . . and then she smiled. She didn't need to get buried under a mound of boards to learn the lesson he'd learned. With her dad and Aunt Debby looking out for her, it was all going to be all right.

She hoped.

When Emily rounded the corner to the ring, she saw all her cousins, Meredith, and Uncle Rick all sitting on the fence rail . . . to watch her lesson?

She sucked in her breath, feeling her cheeks burn, and she opened her mouth to protest—

"Emily!"

She glanced over at her aunt, who was in the ring, then froze.

Her aunt was holding Sapphire. And he was tacked up, ready to be ridden.

But no one was on him.

"What's he doing here?" Her mouth was parched, her hands shaking again. She looked at her dad. "Dad?"

He grinned down at her, his face delighted. "We decided that you need to ride a horse you trusted, and there's no horse you trust as much as Sapphire."

Her mouth gaped. *"My lesson is on Sapphire?"*

He chuckled. "It won't be if you don't get into that ring and get on him."

Tears filled Emily's eyes as she stumbled forward, her vision blurry as she hurried toward Sapphire. She climbed through the rails and rushed into the ring, then came to an awed stop a few feet from him. Afraid it was a mistake or a joke . . .

Then Aunt Debby held out Sapphire's reins to her, a wide smile on her face. "You going to get on or what?"

"Oh, *yes*." Emily snatched the reins, but instead of climbing on, she threw her arms around Sapphire's neck and buried her face in his soft coat. He snorted and stepped sideways, dragging her along. Emily let go and grinned at her aunt. "He wants me to get on."

"Of course he does. Leg up?"

"Definitely!" Emily grasped the saddle and lifted her leg.

"On three. One, two, three—" Aunt Debby hoisted her up and Emily threw her leg over Sapphire's broad back, sinking deep into the leather saddle.

"Oh, *wow*." Emily leaned forward and stroked his neck as Aunt Debby adjusted her stirrups for her, unable to believe she was really on Sapphire. Not sneaking a ride, but really, *truly* allowed to ride him.

Sapphire turned his head to look at her, then lifted his upper lip in a grimace that totally made her laugh. His dark brown eyes were fastened on her, and something inside her chest bubbled with warmth. It was Sapphire. He would take care of her.

Aunt Debby patted her leg. "You're good. Why don't you go warm up?"

Emily tucked her feet in the stirrups and looked

down at the joy in Aunt Debby's eyes. "Thank you."

Aunt Debby winked at her. "Get to work, Emily. We're not here to chat."

Emily giggled and gathered her reins, not at all put off by her aunt's manner. Not anymore. She sank into her heels and lightly pressed her calves to Sapphire's sides.

He immediately moved forward into a rolling walk that was so comfortable and so majestic, just like he was. She glanced over at her audience on the fence rail.

They were all grinning at her, even Kyle. Meredith gave her a thumbs-up, and Emily returned it, and then saw Hercules and Max standing at the edge of the crowd. Hercules was resting his little black nose on the bottom rail, and he was watching her. She blew him a kiss, and he snorted and darted behind Max to hide, then Hercules poked his head beneath Max's belly to peer at Emily. She smiled, realizing that Hercules had found his home with Max, and that he was going to be all right.

Sapphire gave a jig to the right, and Emily laughed as she followed along with him, keeping balance over his broad back. "Even in the ring, you still have to be a troublemaker, don't you?"

He craned his head around to look at her, and she

could have sworn he winked. She knew then she was in for a very spirited ride as only Sapphire could give, and her heart jumped in eager anticipation. "Well, if you're that energetic, let's get going!"

She nudged Sapphire into a trot, sighing with delight as he responded, hopping into action with a trot that was powerful and athletic. His muscles rippled beneath her as he pushed forward. So much strength and energy. So graceful and light as he danced across the ground, his toes barely brushing it. The comparison to Moondance . . . No. There was no comparison. He was . . . he was *everything*.

She glanced over at Aunt Debby, suddenly thrilled that she didn't believe in the eternal warm-up like Emily's old coach, Les, did. "Canter?"

Aunt Debby nodded, a twinkle in her eye. "Go for it."

Emily sat down in the saddle and nudged Sapphire into a canter. Energy rippled through him, his tail swished, and she laughed, knowing exactly what he was going to do before he did it.

She sat up, took a firm grip on the reins and giggled when Sapphire squealed and bolted, trying to get his head down so he could plant a firm buck. "I know you too well, Sapphire." She threw her weight back so he couldn't get his head down. "You're such a troublemaker."

She had Sapphire back under control in seconds, because he'd never really gotten out of control. He swished his tail again and did a tiny buck and then settled back down to a proper canter. She patted his neck, chuckling as he shook his head. "You can't pull that stuff on me, sweetie."

"Nice work, Emily."

She looked over at her aunt, who was leaning on an oxer. "Really?"

Aunt Debby nodded. "You knew what he was doing before he did it, and stopped him. Good job."

Emily heard the sincerity in her aunt's voice and was unable to stop herself from beaming. She'd done right by Sapphire. Proven she was capable of riding him. Maybe it had started out as a pity ride, but now . . . now it was different.

This wasn't going to be the only time she was going to be allowed to ride him. *She'd done it.*

Her aunt lowered the cross rail and pointed to it. "You up for it, Em? No pressure."

Emily looked at the red-and-white-striped rail, and the jump she'd crashed on at the show flashed through her mind. Then Sapphire snorted and pranced sideways,

203

and she remembered she was on him.

On her best friend. Together, they could do it.

She adjusted her reins and nodded. "Let's do it."

Aunt Debby nodded. "Just trot up to it, go up in half-seat and grab his mane. He has much more spring than Moondance, so if you don't hold on to his mane, you're going to get left behind."

"Of course he'd jump bigger than Moondance. He's Sapphire!" She clucked him into a trot and looked ahead to the jump, planning her approach.

She turned and straightened him out. His head came up and his ears went forward, and she felt his body coil beneath her. The jump got closer, and she waited for a flash of fear . . . but none came.

Just total and complete confidence in the horse she was riding and the team they made together.

She rose in her stirrups and grabbed his mane, keeping him straight between her calves. Two more steps . . .

Sapphire exploded into the air, vaulting so high above the cross rail Emily felt like they were flying! She clung to him, gripping his mane and clenching her calves as they sailed through the air, keeping her position and balance perfect as they came down, landing gracefully.

"Keep going," Aunt Debby said. "Canter the vertical in six strides."

Emily looked ahead to the vertical and saw it was bigger than any she'd ever jumped. It wasn't three feet, but it seemed pretty close. With a hit of adrenaline, she directed Sapphire toward the vertical rail, counting his strides as he thundered forward. *Land, one, two, three, four, five, six!* Sapphire vaulted through the air again, sailing so high they almost touched the sky.

They hung in the air for what seemed like hours, and she knew she'd come home. To her family, to Sapphire, to the farm, and to the kind of riding that would fill her soul forever.

Read an excerpt from the third
book in the Running Horse Ridge series!

*E*mily Summers was pretty certain that this was the best moment of her life. The sun was glorious, the sky was a radiant blue, and the air smelled like wood shavings and the baby shampoo she'd used on Sapphire last night. It was utter perfection—so fitting for what was about to happen.

She sank deep into her stirrups, tightened up her reins, and stroked Sapphire's sleek, black coat. "Are you fired up for this or what, beautiful?"

Sapphire snorted and did a little sideways prance. Emily grinned. They were both so ready for this debut.

She watched her new friend at the barn, Meredith Jenkins, and her cousin Alison Neils cantering side-by-side. Their heads were bent toward each other in deep discussion while they warmed up, and they didn't notice Emily's arrival at the practice ring.

They'd be so psyched when they realized Aunt Debby had invited Emily to ride in their lesson with them. It had been less than a month since Emily and her dad had flown in from New Jersey to stay at her aunt and uncle's Oregon horse farm, Running Horse Ridge, and she was already joining a jumping lesson with Alison and Meredith. How cool was that? "We rock," she whispered to Sapphire.

He flicked one ear back to listen, and then flipped his head up and down impatiently.

"I know. I just wanted to savor the moment." Emily sat tall, drew her shoulders back, made sure her wrists were straight, and then nudged Sapphire through the gate. Her chest expanded with pride as they strode into the ring. She was just getting to know Alison and Meredith. She hoped that joining their lesson would totally make them tight and then she would finally have true friends at the barn.

At her command, Sapphire walked purposefully into the arena, his haunches gathered beneath him and his head down in a perfect dressage walk. She grinned, waiting for the reaction of her new friends to the great walk she was making Sapphire do. Running Horse Ridge might be a jumping barn, but even jumper riders could appreciate a quality walk. Maybe they'd even ask for her help in teaching their horses how to walk better. . . .

Alison and Meredith rounded the corner at the end of the ring, heading up the backstretch. All they had to do was glance right and they'd see Sapphire and Emily.

She waited, her heart racing.

And waited . . .

But neither Alison nor Meredith looked in her direction. Emily could hear their excited chatter across the ring.

For a moment Emily's wrists drooped, and then she straightened her hands and urged Sapphire into his long graceful trot, heading right toward them. "Hi, guys! Guess who gets to join your lesson!"

Meredith glanced in her direction and waved, then Alison turned around, saw her, and lifted her wrist in what Emily assumed was a greeting.

Emily waved, but by the time she raised her hand, they were already back to their conversation.

She let out a sigh and cut across the ring to move up next to them. "Did you hear me? I'm in your lesson today!" She urged Sapphire into a canter so she was riding alongside them.

Meredith and Alison stopped talking then. "We heard," Meredith said. "That's cool."

But she sounded distracted, and Emily frowned, settling deeper into her seat as Sapphire shimmied sideways, nearly bumping Meredith's chestnut horse, Halo. "What are you guys talking about?"

"Fourth of July." Meredith glared at Sapphire as he bumped Halo, making Halo swish his tail and take an annoyed stutter step. "We're debating costumes."

"Costumes? You dress up for the Fourth of July?" Sapphire reached over and tried to nip Halo on the ear, and Emily grinned as she tugged his head away. "Stop it, you goof."

But Meredith wasn't smiling. "Don't let him do that, Emily. I've already had issues with Halo biting. I don't want him to start again."

"Keep Sapphire away from Icy," Alison warned. "He's wiggy enough riding this close to Halo. We're practicing for the parade, and I need to get him calm."

"Parade?" Sapphire moved his head suddenly and nudged Halo hard, making Halo jump to the left and bang into Icy.

"Emily!" both girls shouted at her.

Emily felt her cheeks heat up. "Sorry, I was just—"

"Don't ride next to us if you can't control your horse," Alison said, her voice tense as she tried to calm Icy. She'd had Icy for only a few weeks and was still getting used to him. "Go to another part of the ring."

Emily pressed her lips together and turned Sapphire to ride away. He tossed his head and did a little buck, and she let him, even though she knew she shouldn't. "I know, sweetie. You aren't boring like those horses. You can be yourself with me."

She loosened the reins and moved into a half-seat, standing in her stirrups to get herself off Sapphire's back while he cantered. Emily relished the movement of his well-muscled body beneath her, the massive strength and power of him, the sound of his hooves thudding on the dirt.

This was what mattered: being with Sapphire, enjoying the moment.

But she couldn't help stealing a glance across the ring at Meredith and Alison in deep conversation, their horses cantering in perfect control right next to each other.

Emily pulled her gaze away and let Sapphire have the bit. He stretched out, then dipped his head and gave a hard buck, his rear end flying into the air and flinging her out of the saddle. Emily grabbed for his mane as she tumbled forward. "Sapphire!" She lost the reins and clung to his mane, scrambling to get her weight back as he stretched out and increased his speed, racing as if he were in an open field instead of an enclosed ring. If he bucked now, she'd go flying, and she could feel him gather his muscles, aware of her vulnerability. "Hey! Don't you dare try to dump me."

A flash of gray caught her eye, and she looked up and saw Icy and Halo directly in front of her. Sapphire was approaching too fast! Emily shouted a warning, and her friends turned, their eyes widening in horror as they saw Sapphire thunder toward them with Emily clinging to the side of his neck. For a split second they all stared at one another in stunned shock, then there was a squeal of terror and the thud of horseflesh colliding as Emily was surrounded by screaming girls, shrieking horses, and iron-shod hooves slicing through the air right next to her face.

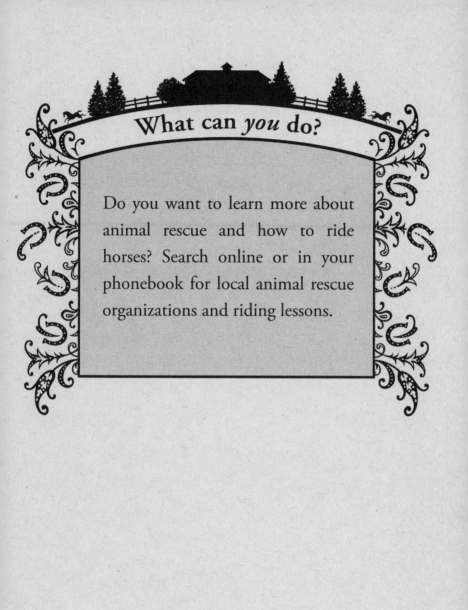

What can *you* do?

Do you want to learn more about animal rescue and how to ride horses? Search online or in your phonebook for local animal rescue organizations and riding lessons.

HEATHER BROOKS loves horses and the outdoors. She says that nothing can compare to galloping free over open range—except maybe writing a perfect sentence. She has been riding all her life and especially enjoys eventing (a sport that includes cross-country, show jumping, and dressage). Heather is also passionate about equine rescue, and many of the equine characters in the Running Horse Ridge books are inspired by real rescued horses.